# MELONHEAD
## AND THE BIG STINK

# MELONHEAD
## AND THE BIG STINK

BY KATY KELLY

ILLUSTRATED BY GILLIAN JOHNSON

DELACORTE PRESS

Text copyright © 2010 by Katy Kelly
Illustrations copyright © 2010 by Gillian Johnson
Photograph on page 212 copyright © 2010 by Shutterstock

Visit us on the Web! www.randomhouse.com/kids

Educators and librarians, for a variety of teaching tools, visit us at
www.randomhouse.com/teachers

*Library of Congress Cataloging-in-Publication Data*
Kelly, Katy.
  Melonhead and the big stink / by Katy Kelly ; illustrated by Gillian Johnson.
    p.  cm.
  Summary: During the summer between fourth and fifth grade, Adam "Melonhead" Melon,
who lives in the Washington, D.C. neighborhood of Capitol Hill, tries to stay out of trouble to
earn a trip to New York City to see the giant "stink flower."
  ISBN 978-0-385-73658-9 (hc)—ISBN 978-0-385-90617-3 (glb)—
  ISBN 978-0-375-89656-9 (e-book)
  [1. Behavior—Fiction. 2. Summer—Fiction. 3. Washington (D.C.)—Fiction. 4. Humorous
stories.] I. Johnson, Gillian, ill. II. Title.
  PZ7.K29637Mg 2010
  [Fic]—dc22
                               2009020078

The text of this book is set in 14-point Goudy.

Printed in the United States of America

10 9 8 7 6 5 4 3 2 1

First Edition

For my sister, Nell Kelly Conroy,
who was born sweet and grew sweeter, in spite of a childhood marked by
inventive haircuts given by overconfident sisters. Such is the price of love.

# 1
# THE LIST OF DOOM

Chair walking is a top skill of mine. Most people can't do it. Bart Bigelow begs me to teach him the Melonhead Method. I tell him, "Number one. I don't plan to chair walk. It just happens. Number two. It only happens for monumental reasons."

Like the last bell on the last day of fourth grade. When it rang I got an unstoppable urge. I had to jump on my chair. With one foot on the edge of each side, I tilted to the right. The left chair leg lifted off the floor. I tipped it forward and did my quick twist. That chair and I were on the move.

"Adam Melon," Mrs. Timony said. "For the last time this year, get DOWN."

"Don't worry," I said. "I'm over the falling stage."

I landed on Kathleen's desk.

"Melonhead!" she screamed.

Jonique shrieked, "You smashed her Early Americans diorama."

"To reens and smithereens," Lucy Rose said.

"I know," I said. "I can feel Pilgrims poking me in the back."

Mrs. Timony rushed over. "Adam, are you hurt?"

"Nope," I said. "But I'm sorry about the diorama, Kathleen."

"I was done with it anyway," she said.

"Send him to Mr. Pitt!" Ashley yelled.

Mr. Pitt is in charge of behavior.

Mrs. Timony clapped her hands to make the class pay attention. "People who have inventions on the back table may go get them. State fair projects are by the door. Do not forget your art portfolios. You are a wonderful class and you are now dismissed."

Everyone yelled and clapped. Most of the boys

stomped their feet. Robinson Gold put her pinkie fingers in her mouth and let out a fierce whistle. I hooted. My best friend, Sam, yelled, "We're official fifth graders!"

The rest of the class left in a rush.

"Adam and Sam," Mrs. Timony said. "It's time to pack up the Miraculous Mesmerizer."

The M.M. was supposed to hypnotize people. It only worked on Lucy Rose. She might have been faking.

Mrs. Timony gave us a bag for the Mesmerizer's marbles.

"Thanks," Sam said. "When we brought the M.M. to school, the marbles escaped on the stairs."

"And Mr. Pitt was behind us," I said. "His legs got sprained."

"I remember," Mrs. Timony said. "Are you boys going to baseball camp again?"

"I can't," I told her. "My mom thinks it gives me dangerous ideas."

"Why would she think that?" Mrs. Timony asked.

"She's against fire," Sam said.

"Most mothers are," Mrs. Timony said. "What does fire have to do with baseball camp?"

"At the end of camp, Coach R.J. juggles flaming baseball bats," I said. "Real fire. Real bats. Five at once. It's the show that beats all shows. Believe me. If you don't, ask Sam."

"Believe him," Sam said.

Mrs. Timony nodded. "I imagine your mom worries that you will be tempted to light baseball bats on fire."

"We would never," Sam said. "You can't go around playing with fire."

"She's also against bat throwing," I said.

"We did try that," Sam said.

"But now I know how to toss bats so I don't give myself a concussion," I told Mrs. Timony.

"Dr. Stroud called it mild, but Mrs. Melon outlawed it," Sam said.

"Mothers can be awfully picky," Mrs. Timony said.

"Can they ever," I said.

Mrs. Timony laughed.

About what, I don't know.

"My mom is picking us up so we don't have to carry the Mesmerizer," I said.

Mrs. Timony lugged the spinning tube parts to the door.

"You're a great teacher, Mrs. Timony," I told her. "You hardly ever panic."

"You are interesting students," she said. "Your ideas don't always work, but they are original. I admire your energy. And, Adam, I've gotten so used to your rowdy celebrations that I may have to ask my husband to stand on a kitchen chair and wiggle."

"I'd like to watch that," I said.

She smiled. "Do something wonderful this summer, boys. Try to stay out of trouble."

"We haven't had one single incident in over two weeks," Sam said.

"The last one was too small to count," I told Mrs. Timony. "The only things that got hurt were Sam's math book, my dad's white socks, and some mangoes."

Since Sam couldn't see over the Mesmerizer's silver reflecting board, I talked him down the steps and led him to the Melonmobile.

"Hop in, fifth graders," my mom said. "We're celebrating at Baking Divas."

The Divas are our personal friends. Also, they're the mom and aunt of our friend Jonique McBee. Sometimes they give Sam and me old cookies for free.

"I'm starving for a Crazin' Raisin bar," I told Mrs. McBee.

Sam picked a BooMeringue.

"Once you have one, you keep coming back for more," Aunt Frankie told us. "Get it?"

My mom got iced tea and a Snow Scone. The snow is sugar powder. We sat at an outside table.

"How was the last day of school?" she asked.

"Bart Bigelow took apart the pencil sharpener," I said. "He dumped it out in Ashley's backpack."

"Ground-up pencil really shows up on yellow," Sam said.

"Poor Ashley," my mom said.

"She kind of deserved it," I said. "She called him Nosepicker."

"I don't know how Mrs. Timony can keep up with twenty-two children," my mom said. "In fact, I don't know how your mom keeps up with two, Sam."

"I'm a pretty easy kid," Sam said.

My mom laughed.

Then she said, "Adam, I have something for you."

"Is it a fossil?" I asked. "Because as soon as I get one, I'm starting a collection."

"No," my mom said. "It's something I made to help you. I want you to keep it with you all summer."

I thought, *Please don't let it be another sunblock carrier.*

It was an index card.

"To make it fun I named it Remind-O-Rama," she said.

"What does it do?" I asked.

"Whenever you get an idea, just check the Remind-O. If you see it, don't do it."

Every sentence was in a different color.

1. NO walking on roofs.

2. NO climbing trees.

3. NO putting things in your nose.

4. NO snakes.

5. NO rodents.

6. NO playing in our yard until after the Capitol Hill House & Garden Tour and Contest.

7. NO haircuts by nonprofessionals.

"There's nothing left," I said.

It's the List of Doom.

Sam got to stay for dinner. We had chicken chunks with mayonnaise. I don't love it but (1) When my dad is home for dinner my mom fixes food he likes, and (2) Compared to the L.O.D., slimy chicken is not the biggest deal.

"Adam, there are lots of other fun things to do," my mom said. "We'll put together a great summer. How does arts and crafts camp sound?"

Like jail.

"Does this mean I can't play with Jimmy Conroy's new white rat?"

My mom shivered. "I'm sorry, darling boy, but rodents are unsanitary."

"Mrs. Conroy is a teacher," Sam said. "She'd only buy a sanitary one."

"Betty," my dad said, "I think it's different when the rat is a pet."

"It's unbearable to think about rodent teeth snapping down on Adam's skin," she said.

"Not to me," I said. "I'd like having a rat scar."

"I think our boy has learned from past adventures," my dad said. "I don't know that he needs a list."

"The Remind-O is to help him make good choices," my mom told my dad.

"Adam," she said to me, "it's for your safety and for my mental health. I won't be able to concentrate on the garden contest, or anything else, if I'm always wondering if you and Sam are keeping company with snakes or stuck in a tree or falling off a roof. I'll admit, I'm a little bit of a worrier."

"My dad says you are a big worrier," Sam said.

"He does?" my mom said.

"Not big like fat," he said to Sam. "Big like a lot. Like you worry a lot. My dad would never call you fat."

"I wouldn't say I'm a big worrier," she said. "I'm just careful."

My dad smiled at me.

"Would it cheer you up to know that we got five hundred ladybugs in the mail today?" my mom asked. "They're going to eat the aphids that are eating my rosebushes."

"May Sam and I see them?" I asked.

"Not now," she said. "Riding around in the mail makes ladybugs hyper. To calm down they have to stay in the refrigerator until tomorrow evening."

My dad looked at my mom and said, "You know, Betty, among us Melons, Adam has the most insect experience."

"Absolutely," she said.

"I believe our son is the man for the ladies," my dad said.

"You're right," my mom told him. "Adam, for the next twenty-four hours you are the official ladybug keeper."

"Really?" I said. "Thanks!"

"Isn't that better than hanging out with a rat?" my mom asked.

"Mom," I said. "Did you know that when you say *rat*, your arm hair jumps straight up? It looks like a little hair forest."

"Lucky thing it's dark brown or nobody could see it," Sam said.

My dad says ladies like compliments.

# 2

# FIVE HUNDRED MISTAKES

This morning I was in my room timing how long I could stand on my head, when I remembered the time our refrigerator got so cold that the eggs froze.

I did one quick flip and jumped down the steps three at a time. I ran through the dining room, slid across the kitchen floor, and yanked open the refrigerator. The box was in between a jar of dill pickles and a jug of maple syrup. The pickle jar was ice cold. The ladybugs had to be shivering.

When I opened the box, it was worse.

They were dead.

"I'm sorry, ladies," I said. I felt lousy.

To check for survivors, I stirred them with my finger.

Good luck struck. One wiggled.

 "Come on, girl," I said. "You can make it."

I gave the box a gentle shake. Nothing. Then a stream of 499 ladybugs flew out of the box. One stayed. It was dead.

The good news was the miracle of ladybug life. The bad news: my mom goes nuts if she sees ONE bug in the kitchen.

I yanked open the back door. "Shoo," I said. "Go outside. Vamoose. Fly."

"Adam?" my mom yelled. "Is that you?"

I didn't expect her to be in the yard.

I ran outside, stood on the porch, and yelled.

"Great news! The ladybugs aren't dead."

She yelled back, "What did you say?"

"Uh, ladybugs are red," I said.

"You thought they came in colors?" she said.

I fake-laughed and raced back inside. I started waving dishtowels to show the bugs the way out. In case they had ears, I gave directions. "This way to the aphid buffet."

My mom was walking up the back steps.

"Don't come in," I yelled. That never works so I had to admit it. "Ladybugs are on the loose."

"Not until this evening," my mom said.

"A few escaped," I said. "But don't panic. I've got them under control."

I don't know why the ladies went for her hair.

My mom flung her head around. "Ack! One is in my ear!"

"Don't panic," I said. "I've got the DustBuster." I sucked up a clump of her hair. "Stay still so I can vacuum them."

My mom put her hands up like she was trying to keep me away.

"Don't worry," I said. "The ladybugs will be fine. They are getting sucked up the chute and landing in the soft inside pocket. They probably think they're at Bugland Amusement Park. After they're caught, I'll give them their freedom. Outside."

"I DO NOT want my hair vacuumed," my mom said, and ran out the back door.

She was dancing around on the back porch when my dad came back from jogging.

"I like your hair that way, Betty," he said. "It's kind of crazy."

"It matches the way I'm feeling," she said.

"Some ladybugs escaped," I said.

"Every ladybug escaped," she said. "They're everywhere."

"Especially the ceiling," I said.

My dad patted my mom's back. "Ladybug cleanup is a father-son job," he said.

It took the rest of the morning. And when we were finally done, we had to discuss the situation. "Well, Sport," my dad said. "Did you learn anything?"

"Ladybugs don't freeze?" I said.

"Think before doing," my dad said.

"Good one," I said.

"Did you tell Mom you're sorry?" he asked.

"Yep," I said. "Plus, I'm going to make up for my mistake. There are still three trays of worms that need to be unloaded."

"Isn't it time for Pop's Second Annual School's Out Extravaganza at Jimmy T's restaurant?" he asked.

Pop is my old friend. He's also Lucy Rose's grandfather. Sometimes he lets me use his saw.

"It's not for an hour," I said. "And worms are waiting."

"You should go early and save a table," my dad said.

"Okay," I said.

I leaned over the porch railing and yelled good-bye to my mom.

"Before you go, bring me the Remind-O," she said.

She wrote on the bottom:

8. NO bugs in the house.

# 3

# I'M A CHUCKLEHEAD

Sam and I nabbed the window booth at Jimmy T's. We like to press our nostrils against the glass. People who aren't expecting to see pig faces jump in horror. But Mrs. T gets mad when we get boogers on the glass, so we just played Jenga with jelly packets until Pop, Lucy Rose, and Jonique got there.

Lucy Rose came in yelling, "Yippee-yi-yo, cow-girl! School's out."

Jonique was behind her. "Pop wrote a song against school," she said.

Pop sang, *"Got no worries, got no fears, because I haven't been to school in thirty-eight years."*

I laughed so hard my ice water came out of my nose. That is an interesting feeling.

A lady in the back booth waved at Pop. "Short and clever. Just like the singer."

The teenager sitting next to her said, "If you need a backup musician, I play guitar."

"Thanks, Justin," Pop said.

"Justin!" I whispered. "That's the guy who called me chucklehead when I was stuck in the tree."

"Maybe he thinks your last name is Chuckle," Jonique said.

"Melonhead, Chucklehead, he could get them confused," Sam said.

"Besides, I completely doubt he remembers," Jonique said.

"The whole neighborhood remembers," I said.

"That's true," Lucy Rose said. "They do."

"That was a small mishap," Pop said quietly. "And it's the only one Justin knows about."

"Wrong," I said. "Whenever he shows up, my life explodes."

"Last month the fence tore a hole as big as a

piece of pizza in the back of Melonhead's pants," Sam said. "He had to walk home holding his butt."

"Guess who was walking right behind me," I whispered.

Lucy Rose and Jonique laughed like girl baboons.

"Justin is a jinx to you," Lucy Rose said.

Mrs. T called across the counter. "What was the best thing about school this year?"

"Music," Justin said. "And science."

"And girls. He *loves* girls," his sister said.

"Math is my top subject," Jonique said.

"Writing and singing are in a tie," Lucy Rose said.

"I like doing experiments," Sam said.

I do too but I didn't say it.

"What was the worst part?" Mr. T asked.

Sam and Jonique and Lucy Rose all said, "Mr. Pitt."

"Man, I remember that guy," Justin said.

"Pop says Mr. Pitt wouldn't get a joke if it bit him on the leg," Lucy Rose said.

"But he would remember it," Pop said. "People always remember when they get bitten on the leg."

Mrs. T came to our table.

"Ladies?" Pop said.

"French toast with cherries flambé," Lucy Rose and Jonique said at the same time.

"We don't set fire to one food," Mrs. T said.

"Well, not on purpose," Mr. T said.

"I know that," Lucy Rose said. "I just adore saying *flambé*."

"I'd like a PBJ," Sam said.

"What about you, kiddo?" Mrs. T asked me.

"Red alert, Melonhead," Sam said. "Justin's family is leaving. Act like you're staring out the window."

Since I couldn't order, I did pig nostrils.

"A BLT for me, please," Pop said.

I sent a supersonic brain-to-brain message to Mrs. T. *Do not talk to me until he is gone.*

"We're off to the pool," Justin's mom said.

I held my breath. In five seconds my close call would be over.

Wrong. Before his mom and sister even got to the door, Justin appeared on the outside of my window.

He tapped the glass in front of my pig nose.

"See you later, Melonhead," he said.

"He remembers you, all right," Sam said.

My face skipped the burning red stage. It went straight to purple.

"So far this is the worst summer of my life," I said.

# 4
# SAVING THE SUMMER

When we walked Pop home, Madam was in the yard, washing Gumbo. He's their size-XXL dog.

"What's the Scoop du Jour?" she asked.

"Melonhead's got misery on account of the Remind-O-Rama," Lucy Rose told her.

"It's the List of Doom," I said. "MY summer is one hundred percent ruined."

Madam read the L.O.D. "I can see how not being able to tromp around on the roof is disappointing, but there's a lot to do in Washington, D.C.," she said.

"I am *not* going to craft camp," I said.

"Of course you're not," Madam said. "You are an inventor, not a crafter."

She gets me.

"Somewhere in Washington there is a fun, non-rule-breaking activity," Pop said. "Use my computer to find it."

"For Melonhead that would be a snake and rodent camp in a tree on the roof," I said.

Pop laughed.

"I know one," Lucy Rose said. "You can go to drama camp with me. They're doing the play of *Seven Brides for Seven Brothers*."

"I am not going to be anybody's husband," I said.

"He'd rather eat lint," Sam said.

"Lint with raw oysters," I said. "And beet juice."

We went inside. I sat in Pop's office chair and turned my back on everybody.

Lucy Rose stood behind me, getting her breath on my head. "Search for *Summer Bonanza*," she said. "Bonanzas are always exciting."

These bonanzas were mostly contests and cruises.

"Try *Marvels in Washington, D.C.*," Jonique said.

Everybody read over my head.

"I agree, the National Cathedral is a marvel," Sam said. "But dancing at Glen Echo is not. Type in *Odd Things.*"

"There are Odd Recipes, Odd Tools, Odd Fruits, Odd Laws, Odd Balls, Odds and Evens. Also somebody who thinks everyone in the government is odd," I said.

Pop walked in. "Try *Odd Events*," he said.

It worked. "Finally something worth doing," I

said. "Who wants to visit the World's Oldest Ham? It's probably covered with mold and other spores."

"I'd rather see the World's Oddest Ham," Sam said. "Keep looking."

"Jackpot!" I screamed.

"This is BETTER than moldy ham," Sam said.

"This is better than flaming bats," I said.

"This is sickening," Jonique said.

"Plus repulsive," Lucy Rose said. "And hideous."

"Exactly," I said.

Pop read it out loud. "The titan arum. Also known as bunga bangkai."

"The grand opening is Saturday, June twenty-second," I said.

"How are you getting to New York City?" Pop asked.

"New York?" I said.

"Home of the titan arum," Pop said. "The New York Botanical Garden."

"I didn't see that part," I said.

"I'd take the lot of you," Pop said. "But Madam and I will be at the beach."

"Got a new plan, Stan?" Sam asked me.

"We have to convince a parent to take us," I said.

"How?" Sam asked.

Pop said, "I'd try asking."

"I'd try earning," Jonique said. "Pay attention to the Remind-O and keep out of situations."

"I do try. They just happen," I said.

Lucy Rose's recommendation was "Be ULTRA-THOUGHTFUL and DESERVING in the extreme. That will make your parents feel like you are utterly delightful."

"Remember to be helpful," Jonique said.

"Utterly helpful," Lucy Rose said. "That shows maturity, which is something you absolutely have to have when you are in New York City. Everybody there is mature like you can't believe."

"Lucy Rose, have you ever been to New York City?" I asked.

"No," she said. "But I'm living there in my adulthood. Plus, I read a story called 'New York, New York, It's Your Kinda Town' in Pop and Madam's magazine and right on the cover it says 'A Guide for Mature People.'"

"We have to be perfect for sixteen days in a row?" Sam asked.

"E-Z P-Z like Parcheesi," Lucy Rose said.

"I stink at Parcheesi," Sam said.

"I don't mind being perfect," I said.

"I feel like I'm getting qualms," Lucy Rose said. "On account of you are the kind of boys that get tempted every minute."

"I have faith in them," Pop said.

Jonique and I could write you a Boys' Improvement Guide," Lucy Rose said.

"B.I.G.," Sam said.

"I say we call it the Boys' Improvement Guide for Acting Responsible Till Stink Sunday," I said.

Pop figured it out right away. Sam laughed so hard his nose ran.

"It's easier to remember BIG," Lucy Rose said.

Jonique pointed to me. "You are severely gross and embarrassing, Melonhead."

That was when Lucy Rose caught on. "What kind of person names their plan BIG FARTSS?"

"A boy," Pop said.

"The second s is silent," I said.

"You'll have to write your own guide," Jonique said.

"No problem," I answered. "I'll do anything to see a one-hundred-pound, twelve-foot flower that smells like dead mammals."

Sam high-fived me. "Ditto for me," he said. "The bunga bangkai is the Big Stink of a Lifetime."

# 5
## FENCEBALL

"You didn't ask your parents yet, did you?" I asked Sam on our walk to Parks & Rec.

"I almost blurted it out," Sam said. "But I made myself wait until we've gotten some good deeds done."

"Good save, Dave," I said. "Ask later."

Sam said, "Problem. The Big Stink is supposed to bloom on a Saturday. My dad has to go to weddings every weekend until September."

Sam's dad is a photographer and weddings are his business. If I were a photographer, weddings would be none of my business.

"But my mom might take us," Sam said.

"Second choice, my mom," I said.

"She is not a bunga bangkai type," he said.

"True, but she's a good sport," I said. "Plus, they probably have tulips or something that moms would like to look at while they wait for their kids."

"Your dad can be our last resort," Sam said.

I felt bad about that.

"He would take us if he didn't have to help Congressman Buddy Boyd get reelected," I said. "He has to go to Florida every five minutes. They have to meet voters. Politics takes a ton of time."

Sam pushed the button that turns the red light green. We always do that, even if we're not crossing the street.

Jonique and Lucy Rose were waiting for us by the swings.

"Asia's on our team," Jonique said.

"Jack Gannon is on ours," Sam said. "He's meeting us at the Crafts Table."

Jack was drawing a cartoon of Mr. Pitt.

"The popping neck veins are realistic," I said.

"I'm adding bursting veins and ear steam," Jack said.

"If Mr. Pitt saw that, he would be scared of himself," Lucy Rose told him.

"It's game time!" Asia yelled.

"Follow me to the extra-high chain-link fence," I said.

"The one that divides the playground from people's backyards," Sam said.

"I never heard of fenceball," Asia said.

"It's not that popular yet," I told her. "We only invented it four days ago."

"It's E-Z," Sam said. "Step One: Throw a tennis ball as high and hard as you can. Step Two: If it gets stuck in the fence, your team gets a point. The other team has to climb up and get it."

"While they're climbing, you get to throw balls at them," I said.

"That's the outstanding part," Jack said.

"I'm scared of climbing high," Jonique said.

"You have to do it," Asia said. "Or we'll lose."

"I'll climb for Jonique," I said.

"Thanks, Melonhead," she said.

"It's okay," I told her. "I like being pelted."

Our team got the first point. Then the girls got four in a row. After that we couldn't catch up. When they had twenty, we had sixteen. Fenceball only goes up to twenty-one.

"It's up to you, Melonhead," Jack said.

I wound my arm around three times and let go.

"It's a fly-by!" Jack screamed.

"How many points for that?" Sam shouted.

"Zero," Asia said. "It totally missed the fence."

I put my pointer fingers in the number one position and did my "We Are the Champions" stomp.

"He deserves ten points," Sam yelled. "No one in the history of

Washington has ever thrown a ball over this fence."

Someone on the other side hollered, "You deserve a good grounding!"

"Who said that?" Jack asked.

Capitol Hill has row houses. The basements are half underground and half overground. That's why first-floor porches are up in the air. I could see the top half of my mom's friend.

Lucy Rose yelled, "Hi, Mrs. Wilkins."

Jonique said, "We know her from when she used to come to Spring Flings at Capitol Hill Arts Workshops. She doesn't anymore."

"Probably because she's a hundred years old," Jack said.

I waved both arms. "Thanks for saying I deserved a good groundin, Mrs. Wilkins!"

"Whatever a groundin is," Sam said quietly.

"I think it's a cookie from Germany," Jonique said.

"It could be a nut," Asia said.

"Come over here," Mrs. Wilkins yelled.

It feels good being a hero.

We raced to the far end of the playground, through the gate, and made a U-turn. I led us down the brick sidewalk into the two-foot-wide alley between the Parks & Rec fence and the backyard fences. It was a long way to go to get to somebody who was only around forty feet away to start with. But climbing up and over would have left Jonique stranded. Plus, last time I climbed over was when I had the pants incident.

"We're here!" I yelled.

Jack shoved his shoulder into the gate. It only moved a foot. I gave him a push.

"Squeeze through the crack," I said. "We'll follow."

There were so many plants I couldn't see ground. Crazy plants. Orange spikes. Purple vines. Yellow puffs. Plus a zillion green leaves. "If Mrs. Wilkins is in the Capitol Hill Garden Contest, your mom doesn't have a chance," Sam whispered.

"Thanks for inviting us, Mrs. Wilkins," I yelled as loud as I could. She might be deaf.

"You're the Melon boy," she said.

"Call me Melonhead," I said.

"Well, Melonhead, do you know what you did?"

"Yes, ma'am," I said.

"What are you going to do about it?" she said.

"I'm still going to be an inventor but I might be a professional athlete on the side," I told her.

She took a big breath. "Do you know what this is, Melonhead?"

It was brown, round, and stringy. All I could think was Please don't let that be a groundin nut.

"It's a huge hair ball," Lucy Rose said. "My Aunt Pansy's cat throws them up."

"It is NOT a hair ball," Mrs. Wilkins said. "It's a root-ball. It used to be connected to this."

35

"Wow!" I said. "I've never seen a flower that's the color of a bruise."

"Why did you pick it?" Jack asked.

"I didn't," she said. "Your ball hit it. Snapped the stem. Knocked the pot flat on the porch floor."

"What a throw I threw!" I said.

"My husband gave me this plant," she said. "I've been nursing it for nine years."

"I'm sorry," I said.

"You could have hit me with that ball," she said. "I could have rolled down the steps and broken my hip. Did you think of that?"

"No, ma'am," I said. "I never think about hips."

"Here's a broom and a bag," Mrs. Wilkins said. "Clean up the dirt. The pot is kaput. Throw it away with the root-ball."

I swept the dirt off the edge of the porch so it fell into the jungle. "Maybe your husband will buy you a new one," I said.

"When you finish, go away," Mrs. Wilkins said.

Then she went inside and shut the door.

"She didn't used to be so utterly crabby," Lucy Rose said.

Sam and I spent the afternoon running up the down escalator at Union Station. We've been practicing since April. So far we've had 176 attempts and zero successes. You have to keep track if you want to get in the Guinness Book of World Records.

# 6
## B.I.G.F.A.R.T.S.S.

We did the Escalator Challenge for an hour. Then a guard asked us to stop.

"Let's walk up Fourth Street," Sam said. "It has a lot of iron fences."

They're good for dragging sticks across.

"Skip the yellow house," I said. "Mrs. Kopp is touchy. She thinks sticks can chip paint."

"Good remembering," Sam said. "She complains to parents."

I patted myself on the back with my stick. "Incident avoided," I said. "Our Boys' Improvement Guide for Acting Responsible Till Stink Sunday is working."

We bought lemonade at Jonny and Joon's.

I lifted the cup to toast. "Three cheers for the B.I.G.F.A.R.T.S.S."

"Four cheers for an incident-free day, Ray."

"We're on a roll, Mole," I said. "Staying out of situations isn't as hard as I thought it would be."

"I'll ask if you can sleep over," Sam said. "We can show maturity tonight and ask my mom tomorrow."

"Deal-E-O," I said. "All we need is a mature idea."

"What's the biggest thing mothers appreciate?" Sam asked.

"Brushing your teeth without being asked," I said. "And they like when you don't smell."

"We smell?" Sam asked.

"Lady noses are like dog noses," I said. "Remember Ashley told the sixth-grade girls that the boys in our class smell like goats?"

Sam smelled his armpit. "What's so bad about goats?"

"Nothing," I said.

"Well," Sam said. "If moms go for showers, I'll take more showers."

"Calm down, Clown," I said. "Don't be drastic. Just rub your dad's deodorant all over yourself. That's just as good. Believe me. I know."

"Also I can help with Julia," Sam said.

"Sign me up. I'm good at inventing baby games."

"Ever since you taught Julia to play plumber, all she does is flush," Sam said. "My mom's watch, my soccer socks, LEGOs, Nilla Wafers, and one of my dad's dress-up shoes have gone down the toilet drain."

"Shoes flush?" I said.

"It got stuck halfway," Sam said. "I saved the day by pulling it out with our salad tongs. My toothbrush was floating inside."

"If I were you, I wouldn't use it anymore," I said.

Sam and I did EVERYTHING for the Alswangs.

"We set the table," Sam said. "Napkins included."

"Thank you," his dad said.

After dinner I told Mr. Alswang, "Thank you for grilling shish kebabs. Except for the vegetables they were delicious."

"That's quite a compliment," Mr. Alswang said.

"You're welcome," I said.

"We'll load the dishwasher," Sam told his mom.

"Do you need your oven cleaned?" I asked. "Or we could grab the dust gobs off the ceiling fan."

"No, thanks," she said. "But I am loving this thoughtful and cooperative attitude."

"That's our motto," I said. "Sam's thoughtful. I'm cooperative."

His parents laughed.

"By the way," Sam said, "since you and Dad enjoy sleeping, we'll watch Julia in the morning."

We turned off the light the first time Mr. Alswang asked.

\* \* \*

In the morning we checked Julia as soon as we remembered.

She was conked out.

"TV time?" I said.

"I can't," Sam said. "My mom read a story about screen time rotting kids' brains. Now I get thirty minutes a day. Julia gets zero. You're lucky. Your parents let you watch TV until your brain turns to sludge."

"True, but you can slide down banisters," I said. "My mom thinks that's as dangerous as war."

"WAR!" Sam said. "Let's play, André! Get the harpoons. I'll open the windows. That way, no broken ones this time."

"That wasn't a harpoon's fault," I said.

"I know," Sam said, "but harpoons aren't that different than baseballs when they hit glass."

Sam's house was built before Mr. Willis Carrier invented air-conditioning. Sam's room has nine windows on three walls. The best parts of the best room are the curtain rods. They are long golden poles that stretch over three windows. They have fake acorns on the ends that are like arrows, sort of. We pulled down the top and bottom curtains. Six rods easily pulled apart to become twelve harpoons.

I scored on my first throw. "You're wounded!" I screamed.

He chucked one at me. I jumped to the side. It flew out the window.

"Harpoon overboard!" Sam yelled.

I leaned out over the sill. "It's in Goodneighbor Dave's bushes," I said.

Pop named them the Goodneighbors after Sam accidentally turned their yard into a swamp. All Dave's wife said was "These things happen." Dave just said, "I was a boy once." The last part was obvious.

By the time all our harpoons were out the windows, Sam had six wounds. Since I had only four, I made a cape out of a curtain, jumped on his trundle bed, and screamed, "Bow to the victor!"

Julia was still asleep when we crept past her room.

We slid down the banister and let ourselves out

the back door. I did my robot voice. "Begin under-cover harpoon rescue."

Only two were in the Rosens' yard. The others were in Sam's. We crawled like army guys across the Goodneighbors' patio. Then we chucked those harpoons and hoisted ourselves over the fence.

"I'll tie them to the harpoon elevator," I said. "You go up and reel them in."

The elevator is just a rope. The harpoons fall out a lot. We're working on a better plan.

Sam and I were in his room setting up for Round Two when we smelled breakfast. "Time to hang the curtains back up," he said. "I'm starving."

"You know what's funny?" I said. "Some curtains are shorter than other ones."

"I never noticed that before," Sam said. "Don't tell my mom. She'll feel bad. She sewed them herself."

Downstairs, Mr. Alswang was making pancakes. Julia was in her high chair. That was lucky, because we had forgotten to recheck her. She was smearing her face with blackberries.

"She's stained, Dad," Sam said.

I held up the toaster so Julia could see herself in the shine.

"I pity," Julia said.

"You can be both," Mr. Alswang said. "Pretty and stained."

He hosed her off with the sink sprayer and dried her with a pot holder.

"She's still pretty purple," Sam said.

"It will wear off by the time she gets married," Mr. Alswang said.

"Where's Mom?" Sam asked.

"She went to yoga," his dad said.

"I need to ask her something," Sam said.

"Would I know the answer?" Mr. Alswang asked.

"Nope," Sam told him. "It's about June twenty-second."

His dad pointed to the calendar on the fridge. "Do you want to help Mom take tickets at the House and Garden Tour? She's in charge of all the money."

"Since when is the tour on June twenty-second?" I asked.

"That's the day of the best yard contest," Sam said.

"It will be a big day for the moms," Mr. Alswang said.

Sam and I studied June 22 on the calendar. *H&G Tour, Chen-Sapperstein wedding 11:00*

AM–*Midnight*. Right there, in black Sharpie marker, was the end of our dream.

"Julia!" Mr. Alswang said. "Berries are for eating, not for hair."

"I wassin," she said.

Mr. Alswang leaned down to take the berries away. Julia rubbed purple smoosh on his head.

"Wassin you air," she said. "An ear."

Mr. Alswang shook his head sideways until the berry blob fell out of his ear. Then he held Julia straight out so she couldn't reach him. "Clean up the dishes, boys," he said. "I'm going upstairs. I've got baby washing to do."

"How are we going to get to New York, Melonhead?" Sam said.

"I'll ask my dad when he gets back from Florida," I said. "But my hopes are not up."

"If we can't go, summer will be worthless," Sam said.

"Don't worry," I said. "We're B.I.G.F.A.R.T.S.S."

Sam laughed. I hooted. Saying that always cheers us up.

# 7

# HOW WAS I SUPPOSED TO KNOW?

Capitol Hill Baptist Church has the smoothest parking lot. It's the number one best place for doing handstands. Lately I've moved up to handwalking. Four handsteps is my record. Today I couldn't get past three, so after an hour, I gave up.

My mom was on the front porch.

"Daddy is waiting for us to call him at his hotel," she said.

"Super-duper, Paratrooper," I said. "I have something to ask him."

She put the phone on speaker so we could both hear. When he answered I said, "Hot diggity, Dad! How's Florida?"

"Florida is fine," he said. "But Mom got a call from Mrs. Papadopoulos. I got a call from Mom."

Usually when calls are going around, it means I'm in a situation. "Don't worry, Dad," I said. "I've been one hundred percent perfect with zero situations. I haven't even SEEN Mrs. Papadopoulos."

"She called about Winnie Wilkins's plant," my mom said.

"That was NOT my fault," I said. "My arm turned supersonic with no warning."

"Adam," my mom said. "You have to be more careful. I live in fear of the neighbors calling."

"Really?" I asked.

"Not real fear, but I do get anxious," she said. "I never know what they are going to tell me. Every time I see Mrs. Lee she mentions the Marshmallow Fluff incident."

"Still?" I said. "That was over a month ago."

"Betty," my dad said. "We can't move forward if we're looking back."

"You're right," my mom said.

"Sport," he said. "That plant was precious to Mrs. Wilkins."

"Sam kept the root-ball," I said. "Mom can re-grow it."

"Even if I could, parents can't fix kids' mistakes," my mom said.

"Here's the deal," my dad said. "You are going to spend two hours doing chores at Mrs. Wilkins's house on whichever three afternoons she chooses."

"I don't think she wants me back," I said.

"I've already talked to her," he said. "You start tomorrow."

"I hope she wants me to fix a toilet," I said. "Or spackle a ceiling. Or take down a wasps' nest."

"What?" my mom said.

"There was no mention of plumbing repairs, Betty," my dad said. "Or wasps. He'll be moving boxes."

"I like carrying heavy stuff," I said. "But I just thought of something. I might not feel comfortable being alone with Mrs. Wilkins."

"You're not supposed to be comfortable," my dad said. "You're supposed to work hard and be polite."

"Personal responsibility, right?"

That is a top topic of his.

"Exactly right, Sport," he said.

"We'll call after dinner to say good night," I said.

"Hold on," my mom said. "We have to discuss the Alswangs' curtains."

"Why did you and Sam take them down?" my dad asked.

"We do it all the time," I said.

That was not a good answer. Explaining about the harpoons made things worse.

"You were LEAPING around next to OPEN SECOND-STORY WINDOWS?" my mom said.

"You're the one who's always saying get exercise," I reminded her.

"How did the curtain rods get bent?" my dad asked.

"Maybe when it landed at the Goodneighbors'," I said.

My mom sucked in her breath. "Did you harpoon a Goodneighbor?"

"They weren't in the yard," I said. "We checked."

You would think I'd get praised for thinking ahead. I didn't.

"I feel like I made a lot of mistakes in two days," I said.

"I feel like that too," my mom said.

"What did YOU do?" I asked.

She looked at me.

"Oh, you mean my mistakes," I said.

She made a little smile.

"What did you learn from this, Sport?" my dad asked.

"The top curtains are longer than the bottom curtains," I said. "Or the other way around."

"What else?" my dad asked.

"Don't throw curtain rods out windows," I said.

"Think before you do," he said.

"Think before I throw curtain rods out the window?" I said.

"Think before you do anything," he said. "Ask yourself, 'Is this a good idea?' "

"Check your Remind-O," my mom said. Then she interrupted herself. "Adam, you are covered with bruises!"

She told my dad, "He is COVERED with bruises!"

"Sport?" my dad said.

"Only two," I said. "This one is just dirt."

I spit on my knee. "Look," I said. "One smear and it's gone."

"How sharp are those curtain rods?" my mom asked.

"Not too sharp," I said to calm her. "The bruises could be from flying tennis balls. But don't worry. There's nothing sharp on tennis balls."

"You got hit with tennis balls?" she asked.

"It's hard to dodge them when you're climbing," I explained. "Lucy Rose has good aim."

"Lucy Rose hit you with balls? On purpose?" my mom asked.

"We all hit each other," I said.

"You fought?"

"It wasn't a fight," I said. "It was a game."

"Hitting is NOT a game," my mom said.

"Sometimes it is," I said.

"Bruises fade, Betty," my dad said.

"That's true, Mom," I said. "If they didn't my entire body would be brownish purple."

"Is there anything else we should talk about?" my dad asked.

"I have a question," I said.

"Let's hear it," he said.

"Never mind," I said. "I'll ask when you get home."

When the curtain and fenceball situations are off his mind.

"I love you both," my dad said.

"Come home soon," my mom said, and hung up.

"I'm sorry," I told her.

"I know," she said.

Then she wrote on the L.O.D.:

9. NO Harpoons.

10. NO beating each other with tennis balls.

She swabbed my bruises with arnica gel. "It could stain," she said. "Sit on a plastic chair in the basement until it dries. You can call Mrs. Alswang while you wait."

These are Pop's Apology Rules. I use them a lot.

1. Mean what you say.

2. Get to the point.

3. Don't dress it up with fancy words.

"From now on I'm thinking before doing," I told Mrs. Alswang. "That way, I won't be tempted to throw your curtain rods ever again. Well, I will be but I'll stop myself."

"I appreciate that," she said.

I hung up and the phone rang.

"News flash!" Lucy Rose said. "*Grounding* is my Word of the Day for tomorrow, but since it is concerning you, I'm telling you now."

"Okay," I said.

"Grounding is when your punishment is staying at home while your friends go out and have a hilarious time," she said.

"I got reverse grounding," I told her. "Instead of staying in my house I'll be in Mrs. Wilkins's house."

"Yipes," she said.

She is good at saying what you are feeling.

"Bye," I said.

"Wait," she said. "There is another kind of grounding. It has to do with electricity."

"I'd like that consequence," I told her.

"I know that," she said. "But you'll have to lump the one you got."

# 8

# CHORE BOY

Being alone with Mrs. Wilkins haunted my mind all morning. At lunchtime I figured out what to do.

I got to her house at 1:22. I sat on the steps. At 1:34 the door flew open.

"You're late," Mrs. Wilkins said.

"I was here," I said.

"It doesn't count unless you ring the bell," she said.

"Mrs. Wilkins," I said. "How about I get Sam and Jack to help? For free."

She stared so hard I had to look down. Her shoes were black and squishy-looking.

"One boy is one boy," she said. "Two boys is half a boy. And three boys is no boy at all."

"Does that mean the more boys there are the less work gets done?" I asked.

"That's exactly what it means," she said.

"So the answer is no?" I asked.

"Yes," she said, "it's no."

Lucy Rose calls Mrs. Wilkins's voice gruff. If that means a mix of grumpy and rough, she's right.

"What do you want me to do?" I asked.

"Stop slouching and go up to the attic," she said.

"Really?" I said. "This is my lucky day!"

"I don't care for sarcasm," she said.

"I might not either," I told her. "What is it?"

"It's when you say the opposite of what you mean, like, 'This is my lucky day.'"

"But I do mean it," I said. "I've never been in an attic. My mom says I could fall through the floor."

"Why would you do that?" Mrs. Wilkins asked.

"She thinks attic floors are old and weak," I said.

"Nonsense," Mrs. Wilkins said. "People think that about me and I'm perfectly capable."

"How old is your house?" I asked.

"It's one hundred and eleven years old."

"You'll be dead when you're that old," I said.

"Possibly," she said. "We'll have to wait and see."

"Okay," I said.

"I suppose you're hungry?"

"I'm always hungry, but don't worry, I bring pockets full of cereal wherever I go."

"I wasn't worrying," she said.

"Point me to the attic," I said.

"It's where all attics are," she said. "Up. But first put my armchair in the hall so I can sit while I'm yelling at you."

"You're not coming up?" I asked.

"And break my hip?" she asked. "No, thank you."

"What am I doing up there?"

"Job One is to find my albums," she said.

I went up two steps at a time.

"Watch it," Mrs. Wilkins said. "I don't have time to take you to the hospital for a broken neck."

She has bones on the brain.

"It's dark up here," I said. "I can't see. Also it smells like old paper."

I was thinking it was creepy when something floaty, like a wisp, dashed across my face. I jumped and bumped into something worse. I grabbed it. It had a waist. I let go fast. It ran backwards.

"What are you hollering about?" Mrs. Wilkins yelled.

I walked toward the steps. Another wisp swooped across my neck.

"Something is after my head," I said.

"Maybe I've got bats in my belfry," she said. She laughed like that was funny.

"Does a lady live up here with the bats?"

"I don't know," she yelled. "I haven't been up there in years."

I felt my neck hairs spring up like they were covered with static electricity.

"Wave your hands around," Mrs. Wilkins yelled. "You'll find the light."

I am no chicken but I do not like grabbing bats or bodies in the dark. "Do I have to?" I asked.

"For pity's sake, Melonhead," she said. "Find the string. Pull it. The light will turn on."

"I never heard of a light that works by string," I said.

It helped to think the wisp might have been the string. Or a bat.

"That took long enough," Mrs. Wilkins yelled. "What do you see?"

"Everything anybody could want," I said.

"Don't go wanting it," she said. "It's mine."

"I didn't mean I wanted it," I said. "I meant it's interesting. I found the lady."

"That's my sewing mannequin," she said.

"It looks like a womankin," I said. Then I felt embarrassed. I was glad she couldn't see my ears. I couldn't either but I knew they were red.

"She was my dummy. I used to make all my own clothes," Mrs. Wilkins said.

I guess she's called a dummy because she has no head.

"I was glamorous when I was young," Mrs. Wilkins said.

I did not know what to say about that.

"What do you see that's useful?"

"Working-man boots," I yelled. "Old trunks, a turquoise coat, skis, and a doll crib. There's a beach umbrella and a big mirror in a curly gold frame."

"Don't touch the mirror," she said. "With your gift for breaking things we'll be wallowing in bad luck."

How did she know I was touching it?

"You'd better not be eating that junk cereal up there," she yelled. "You'll draw bugs."

It was like she had X-ray vision.

"What's in front of you?" she hollered.

"Boxes that say 'Franklin's Notes.' "

"Stay away from them," she said. "They're important."

"There's a pile of Tintin books by the railing," I yelled.

"They belong to my youngest son, Thomas. He and his wife live in Bolivia."

"If I ever move to Bolivia the first thing I'll do is get a llama," I said. "Do they have one?"

"Not that I know of," she said.

"Here's something great!" I said.

"Albums?" she said.

" 'Andy's Rock Collection,' " I said.

"Andy is my middle son. He lives in Egypt. He's an archaeologist," she said.

"Has he dug up anything good?" I yelled.

"No mummies, if that's what you mean," she said.

It was.

"Stop with the questions," she said.

"Some boxes don't have labels," I said.

"Open them. Carefully."

"How will I know when I find the right box?" I said.

"It will be full of albums," she said.

"Are you being sarcastic?" I asked.

"No," she yelled. "I'm being impatient."

"I found an ancient doll," I said.

"It was my mother's. Then it was mine. Then it was my daughter's. I'm saving it until Molly has a baby," she said.

"Hey, here's a picture of a lady sitting on an airplane wing," I said.

"That's no lady," she said. "That's me."

That was the second time she laughed like she'd told a hilarious joke.

"Whose plane are you sitting on?" I yelled.

"It's my plane," she yelled.

"Were you rich?" I hollered.

"We had enough," she said.

"Who actually drove the plane?" I said.

"I did, of course. I'm a pilot," she said.

I jumped down the steps so fast I landed on my knees, right in front of her chair. "Holy moly! Where did you learn to fly?"

"In Africa," she said. "My husband was a scientist."

"Did he quit?"

"No," she said. "He died. But not until much later."

"Are you sad about not having a husband?" I asked.

"Do you want to hear about the plane or do you want to ask questions?"

"Hear," I said.

"When we were first married my husband took a job in Madagascar."

"Doing what?" I said. "Sorry. I forgot about not asking."

"He was an entomologist."

"Bug expert is my second choice of a job," I said.

"Who knew you had a brain in that head?" she said.

"Do entomologists get paid or do they just work for the thrills of it?"

"Both," she said. "When we were young my husband spent most of his time collecting in the jungle."

"You mean the rain forest?" I asked.

"In those days we called it a jungle," she said.

I was filled with questions but I stopped myself.

"Sometimes I went into the *rain forest* with him," she said. "Every week he'd pack up a box of dead insects. I'd drive half a day to the post office and airmail them to the Smithsonian museums here in Washington."

"I bet I've seen his bugs," I said.

"Uh-hum," she said. "I'd spend the other half of the day driving back. One day I decided it would be easier to fly. I found a bush pilot to teach me. I took myself across the channel and to Africa. Later, I took the kids. We flew all over the place. That's probably what makes them want to live so far away now."

"You had a big life," I said.

"Yes," she said. "I did."

"Were you always in Madagascar?"

"No," she said. "Andy was born in Brazil. Molly was born in Papua New Guinea, Thomas in Venezuela. Then Mr. Wilkins got a job at a museum in Rome, so we moved to Italy. We traveled all over Europe. Now, back to the attic. Leave the picture here."

"I have an important question," I said.

"I'll answer when you're off work," she said. "Go upstairs."

"You have a load of fuzzy purple curtains," I yelled down to her.

"I never liked them," she said.

So I figured it was fine to wipe my sweat on them.

I found a lot more things that weren't what she wanted.

At 3:07 Mrs. Wilkins said, "What's your question?"

"Did you ever see the bunga bangkai?"

"No," she said.

"You must be disappointed," I said.

"Bunga bangkais are no bed of roses, you know."

I had to hoot over that. "There's one that's going to bloom in New York," I said. "I'm going to see it." Somehow.

"Bully for you," she said.

"You should fly yourself to see it," I said.

"Ha! I gave up my pilot's license years ago," she said. "And my plane."

"Why would you do that?"

"I don't have anywhere I want to go," she said.

"There are millions of places worth going to," I said. "Exciting places."

"Then you go," she said. "I'm fine right here. I've got all I need. Grubb's drugstore sends my medicine. My groceries get delivered. L.L. Bean ships me clothes. Almost everything comes to me. Including you. If doctors still made house calls, I'd be set."

"Do you visit your kids?" I asked.

"I can't hop halfway around the world on a whim," she said. "I have responsibilities. Without me, my husband's plants would die."

"You could go for walks," I said. "Some days this neighborhood is fascinating."

"Don't tell me what I should do," she said. "I'm old. I've seen plenty of the neighborhood."

"Things change," I said. "People paint their houses. Stores open. The Mannixes almost always have a new baby."

"What's new to you is a rerun to me," she said.

"Once I found a snake in the park," I said.

"I've seen enough snakes," she said.

"When the Supreme Court judges are voting on something big, people march around in front and wave signs. Sometimes, if they're on different sides, they yell at each other. You can't say that's not interesting."

"Come back Tuesday," she said. "Be on time."

Mrs. Wilkins called me back before I got past the Papadopouloses' house. "They're called justices, not judges," she said.

When I got home my mom asked, "How did it go?"

"Better than I thought it would," I said.

"I told you Mrs. Wilkins was nice," my mom said.

"Not really," I said. "But she's interesting."

# 9

# THE ANSWER

Sam's dad dropped him off after supper.

"Your yard is looking like a winner, Mrs. Melon," Sam said.

"Thank you, Sam," she said. "I'm using sea grasses and candy-cane phlox to create what my gardening book calls Areas of Interest."

"I'm interested," Sam said.

You could call that lying or you could call it being polite.

"I'm interested in hearing the question you and Adam have for Mr. Melon," my mom said. "Adam won't give me a clue."

"When you hear it, you won't believe it," Sam told her.

"He won't get home until late tonight," she said. "But you can tell him first thing in the morning."

It took Sam and me forever to get to sleep.

My excitement woke me up. Me jumping back and forth between our beds woke up Sam.

"It's time," I told him.

"I'm starving," Sam said.

We drank half a carton of orange juice and took turns spraying whipped cream in our mouths.

"Guess what I feel coming? B.I.G. F.A.R.T.S.S.," Sam said. I laughed so hard whipped cream sprayed out of my mouth and landed on the window.

"Breakfast in bed," Sam said. "Very thoughtful."

"First we ask," I said. "Then we serve. I don't want my dad to get distracted by food."

Sam carried the juice. I carried the bowls.

"Congratulations to us," Sam said. "Twelve steps. Zero spills."

"Leave breakfast right here on the hall floor," I said. "Also, don't count on a yes."

"I'm ready, Freddie," Sam said.

"We rock, jock," I said. "Remember, show enthusiasm."

In one smooth second I knocked, opened the door, and turned on the light.

My dad sprang up like he was in an ejector seat. My mom squeaked, "What's wrong?"

"It's six-twenty-seven in the morning!" my dad said.

"I knew you'd want to know the news," I said.

My dad grabbed the remote control and started pushing buttons. "Did something happen in Florida? A hurricane? A flood?"

"More important," I said.

Sam was staring at my mom like she was the Mesmerizer. Her sleeping mask was pushed up on her forehead. Wrinkle-removing stickers were on the sides of her lips and eyes. Her mouth snapped into a pink rubber-band O. That made a lip sticker pop off. One side of her mouth turned droopy.

"What is it?" she asked in her panic voice. "Even in my sleep, I knew something was wrong!"

"Calm down, parents!" I said. "It's not bad news! It's the greatest news of our lives. Especially your life, Dad."

My mom exhaled.

"Tell us," my dad said.

"We have to go to the bunga bangkai," I said. "It's in New York."

"Are you nuts?" my mom said. "You boys are far too young to go to a nightclub."

Sam laughed. "It's not a nightclub."

"It's a flower," I said.

"You woke us up to tell us about a flower?" my dad asked.

"It was now or never," I said.

"Now, never, or after we got up," my mom said.

"But you said we could tell Dad first thing in the morning," I said.

My dad mashed his pillow back into sleeping shape and said, "Good night."

My mom said, "I have to admit it. I am pleased to hear that Adam shares my love of plants."

"Mostly, I'm interested in the bunga bangkai," I said.

"It sounds exotic," she said.

"It's red with wavy chartreuse edges," I said. "With yellow in the middle."

"I love red," my mom said.

"Some are so red they're almost black," Sam said.

My dad put the pillow over his face.

"It's the hugest flower in the world," Sam said.

"What could be lovelier?" my mom said.

"In the jungle it can get TWELVE FEET TALL and SIX FEET WIDE," I said, loudly. "In captivity, over six feet."

"One flower?" my mom said.

"One flower that weighs a hundred pounds," Sam said.

"It only blooms every seven years!" I said.

"That's some wait," my dad mumbled.

"And, get this, the bunga bangkai only blooms for two or three days, tops," I said. "Then it keels over dead."

"It must be beautiful," my mom said.

"No," I said. "It's hideous."

"And hot," Sam told her. "It has a temperature of a hundred degrees."

"In people, a hundred degrees is a fever," I said.

"Why do people want this flower?" my mom asked.

"Because it smells," I said.

"Well, that makes sense," she said. "One flower-would be enough to make gallons of perfume."

"If you like perfume that smells like dead mammals," I said.

"Mixed with rot," Sam said.

"Putrid dead mammals, plus rot, plus spoiled food," I said.

"Did you hear that?" my mom asked my dad. "It must be the worst plant on earth."

"That's why it would be a tragedy to miss it," I said.

My dad peeked out from under his pillow. My mom's mouth looked stunned. I could see dangling tonsils.

"Sport," my dad said. "New York is a five-hour drive from here."

"That's not so far if you consider where the bunga bangkai came from," I said. "We could have to go to Indonesia and scout around the rain forests. Even then, we might not find one. The Big Stink is rare."

"No one is going to Indonesia," my mom said. "Rain forests are full of snakes."

She has a sore spot for snakes.

"Getting to see it in the USA is a great deal," I said. "The next chance isn't for three years and that titan arum will be even further away—in San Diego."

"A trip to New York would be a great chance for you to spend time with Adam," my mom said.

"And me," Sam said.

"When does the Big Stink bloom?" my dad mumbled.

"In twelve days," I said.

"We have to be first in line," Sam said. "The stink gets weaker after thirteen hours."

My dad patted my mom's back. "Betty, this is a job for Supermom," he said.

"It's on the same day as the garden contest," I said.

My mom smiled at my dad. "Back to you, dear."

"I'll check my date book when I get up, Sport," my dad said.

"I'll get it off your bureau," I said.

My mom laughed.

"Great news, Dad," I said. "You have three blank days right when we need them!"

He looked. "So I do," he said.

"So we're going?" Sam asked.

My dad studied the pages before and after.

"You bet," he said.

I could have fallen over from shock and happiness.

"Are you one hundred percent sure?" I asked.

"I am," he said. "The Congressman will be on vacation. That's the one thing he doesn't need me for."

I hugged him hard. "Thank you, Dad!"

"Mr. Melon," Sam said. "You are king of the world."

My mom squeezed my dad's hand and said, "Thank you, honey."

I hugged his ankles. "I'll do favors for you for the rest of my life," I said.

"Happy boys are enough thanks, Sport," my dad said. "Although I'd be grateful if you would keep far away from situations that alarm your mother."

"No problem," I said. "We're following B.I.G.F.A.R.T.S.S."

"Following what?" my mom said. She looked like she was going to throw up.

"Boys' Improvement Guide for Acting Responsible Till Stink Sunday," Sam said.

My mom does not think B.I.G.F.A.R.T.S.S. are

hilarious. She won't even say the word *fart*. My dad says ladies don't appreciate that word.

"It's the reason we haven't had one single situation except the harpoons," I said.

Sam opened the door.

"And fenceball," I said. "But like you said about doing tricks on Grandma, those days are behind us."

I stepped into the hall without looking.

Sam yanked the door shut. "You're stepping in the cereal bowl!" he said.

"I know," I whispered. "Believe me. I've got cereal squish between my toes."

Sam pulled off his T-shirt and mopped up the milk. I wiped my foot on my pajama leg. "We'll give my dad the full bowl," I said. "My mom doesn't eat that much anyway."

I crept back into their room and around the bed so I was standing next to the pillow that was covering my dad's head. Sam stood next to my mom.

"Presenting Breakfast in Bed." I used my ringmaster voice.

My dad yanked his pillow off his head. The pillow hit the bowl. That made my thumb slip. That made a wave of milk and Cheerios land on his face.

You could tell by his scream that he was grumpy.

"Don't feel bad about spilling it, Dad," I said. "It could happen to anybody."

"I'll be in the shower," he said.

Sopping up the milk hardly took a second. Most of it had soaked into the mattress.

"We'll go now, Mom," I said. "Sleep."

"Hold on," she said. "Bring me clean sheets from the linen closet and your Remind-O."

She got a pencil out of her night table drawer.

11. NO waking parents before 7:30.

12. NO meals in beds.

"Don't forget about your cereal, Mrs. Melon," Sam said.

"I would never," she said, and ate a spoonful. "Very tasty."

We carried the milky sheets to the laundry room. Even though my dad said he'd take us, we're still being helpful.

# 10

# SIX HOURS EARLY

Sam's grandmother Mimi took him to the International Spy Museum on Tuesday. Since I wasn't invited, I went to Mrs. Wilkins's house. She was on the porch.

"You're six hours early," she said.

"I know," I said.

"Fine with me," she said. "I'm always up. When you get old you don't sleep."

"When you're young, parents make you go to bed," I said.

"The world can be a backwards place," she said.

"What am I doing today?" I asked.

"Back to the attic," she said.

I stopped. The airplane picture was on the hall table. I wished I were sitting on that wing.

"If I wanted someone to stand around all day, I would buy a statue," she said.

She sat on her hall chair. I yelled my finds. "Baskets!"

"Don't care," she said.

"Red-and-orange quilt."

"Leave it."

"Envelopes with pictures of people wearing crazy costumes?"

"What costumes?" she yelled.

"This one has a drawing of a lady wearing a vest. It's longer than her skirt. She has white boots and purple ball earrings. I can't explain the hat," I yelled. "What's she supposed to be?"

"That outfit was a smash hit," Mrs. Wilkins yelled. "There's a sewing pattern in the envelope. I made it and wore it in Paris."

"Are you being sarcastic?" I yelled.

"No," she said. "I needed something chic for a lunch honoring my husband. He won an award for finding a new species of poison frog."

"I didn't know he was famous," I said.

"He wasn't," she said.

"You'd get fame if you discovered a poison frog," I shouted. "Believe me."

"Believe me," she said. "You don't. You get a nice lunch and people make speeches about you."

"Are you telling me people can get famous for doing useless ballet but not for finding a new animal?"

"I am telling you that," she said. "I'm also telling you to get back to business."

"Are you interested in yarn?" I hollered.

"I'm interested in albums," she said.

On top of the bookcase there was a box big enough to hold plenty of albums. To reach it, I stood on a rickety rocking chair and leaned forward until I could grab the cardboard edges with the ends of my fingers. Then, with no warning, the chair curled backwards. Then I did. The box flew over my head. It landed upside down.

"Did you break something?" Mrs. Wilkins yelled.

"Don't worry!" I said. "I'm all right. I've got strong hips."

"I'm asking about my belongings," she said.

"It was a box of party hats," I said.

"Let me see the damage," she said.

They looked fine to me but Mrs. Wilkins tried on every hat. "I'll keep this one down here to make sure you don't destroy it," she said.

It looked like a cake covered with silver glitter. Red ruffles were on the bottom. A peacock feather poked out of the top.

"Did you wear that to the frog lunch?" I asked.

"No," she said. "I wore it for other special occasions—New Year's Eve, my kids' birthdays, breakfast on Valentine's Day."

"Why did you stop?" I asked.

"Everyone grew up," she said. "Now, go pick up the confetti you left all over the attic floor."

How does she know these things?

"Hey," I shouted. "Here's a box of high heels. You don't have to wear squishy shoes anymore."

"Do you want lunch?" she asked.

"It's ten-thirty," I said.

"I listen to my body and my body says it's lunchtime," she said.

"I wish everybody did that," I said.

"Keep working. I'll call you when it's ready."

When I came down there were two bowls of strawberry ice cream on the table.

"What's for lunch?" I asked.

"You're looking at it," she said.

"Really?"

"Of course really," she said.

"At home I can't eat dessert until I eat protein."

"If I did that I wouldn't have room for ice cream," she said.

"My dad's taking Sam and me to see the bunga bangkai," I said.

"Take pictures," she said.

"What do you do if you finish your ice cream and you're still hungry?" I asked.

"I have seconds," she said.

So we did.

"Can you water the backyard without killing more plants?" she asked.

"Sure," I said.

She sat in a green chair on the porch and looked down at the yard. "I'm watching you," she said.

"Are you in the garden contest?" I asked.

She laughed like a hyena with fleas. "I don't need a prize to tell me I have a great yard. Besides, where would the judges stand?"

"That's a relief," I told her. "My mom really wants to win."

"What kind of garden does she have?"

"She calls it an English garden," I said. "I don't know how that's possible in America."

"Boring," Mrs. Wilkins said.

"No, it's not," I said.

She pointed. "Sweet peas and roses fade away next to that Snow Fountain dwarf weeping cherry tree."

The tree was short, crooked, and lumpy. "It's nice," I said. "But it can't beat the Big Stink."

"I agree," she said. "Finish watering. And I'll see you tomorrow."

"Before I go, may I see the frog?" I asked.

"It's not like I still have it," she said. "It was poison."

"If I found a poison frog I wouldn't be giving it away," I said. "Believe me."

"The funny thing about the discovery is it was an accident," she said. "Mr. Wilkins was tracking Iguazu butterflies. When he looked down, the frog was sitting on his shoe."

"Lucky he wasn't barefoot," I said.

# 11

# THE BACKFIRED PLAN

"May Sam and I have a Pop-Tart feast in the back-yard?" I asked.

"Come on down," my mom said.

I did not mean to step on the trowel and send it flying. "Be careful," she said. "You scared me to death." I don't know why. Sam was the one who almost got a trowel in his eyeball.

"We'll plant those flowers for you," Sam said.

"Thank you," my mom said. "But cosmos are delicate."

"Do you want any holes dug?" I asked.

"Right now the yard is a one-woman job," she said. "Maybe Sam's mom needs help."

We stuffed
Pop-Tarts in our
back pockets and
headed off to our
E-Z P-Z shortcut.

It starts by climbing over the Reeds' wooden
fence. We ran through their backyard and squeezed
through the bars of Miss Brook's iron fence.

My head got stuck
but Sam shoved it
through. We jumped
over the Sullivans'
mini-pond. Then we
took a break so Sam could
wring out his socks and I could
pull fence splinters out of my stomach.

When we got to Sam's house I announced,
"Help is here, Mrs. Alswang!
You relax and enjoy your
laundry."

"We'll babysit Julia
in the backyard," Sam
said.

"Grand idea," his mom said. "That will keep her away from toilets."

The first thing Julia did in the backyard was pull up lettuce and examine the roots. Then she said, "Peensy pider."

Sam sang. I acted out the Teensy Weensy Spider climbing up the garden spout. Only since I don't know what a garden spout is I used the drainpipe. After about thirteen times I said, "Think of something new, Lou. This is getting boring. Even for Julia."

"E-yi-E-yi-O!" Julia said. "Moo-moo ear."

"I've just got the greatest B.I.G.F.A.R.T.S.S.," Sam said.

"Pig fars," Julia sang.

"My mom wants my dad to paint the yard furniture," Sam said. "My dad wants her to find somebody who likes to paint."

"She just found two of them," I said.

"Watch Julia," Sam said. "I'm going for supplies."

I lay down on the grass and put Julia on my feet

and raised her in the air. "You're a baby airplane," I told her. "Flap your wings."

Her favorite part is crash landings.

Sam came up the outside basement steps with a screwdriver, a can of paint, and two rollers. "Ready?" he said.

"Nope. Because I've been thinking before acting," I said. "Luckily, because we could have had a catastrophe."

"What did you think?" Sam asked.

"We need a drop cloth," I said. "That way, no paint on the grass."

"You are a brainiac," Sam said.

After we spread the blue-and-white cloth Sam found, he pulled a mooshed peach out of his pocket. "Here, Julia," he said. "Sit on the step and eat."

"Nose it," she said.

"Yes, sit," Sam said.

I grabbed Froot Loops from my pocket and made a baby pile on the steps.

"Fooloos!" Julia said.

"Good girl," Sam said to Julia. "Good bribe," he said to me.

"Ready, Freddie?" I said.

"Let's go, Moe," Sam said.

By Chair Number Two we were a two-man painting factory. Julia was biting her peach and spitting out the skin.

"This would go even faster if we didn't have to get up every time we need to get paint," Sam said.

"Invention Alert," I said. "I need your skateboard. And a bungee cord."

"Bunny boor?" Julia said.

I put it together and rolled it across the drop cloth to Sam. "Introducing the Paintmobile," I said. "Two minutes to make, infinity minutes saved."

"At least," Sam said, and rolled it back.

"When I have money I'm going to motorize it," I said. "You'll push a button on the remote control and the paint will come to you."

"People would pay us to paint stuff," Sam said. "Especially if we babysat their kids at the same time."

"Whoa!" I said. "The Paintmobile almost crashed into that chair leg."

"Help me haul the wet chairs," Sam said.

I said, "No sweat, Claudette."

"My dad says if you keep your work area clean you won't have accidents," Sam told me.

"Good thing you remembered," I said.

We dragged the chairs across the grass and left them under the porch, next to the bikes.

"These chairs look brand-new," I said. "Your mom is going to go nuts when she sees them."

"Now for the table," Sam said. "You do the legs. I'll do the top."

"Dooda op," Julia said.

"Have you ever heard of Olympic speed-painting?" I asked.

"No," Sam said.

"You have now!" I said. "And I'm going for the gold."

I got underneath and rolled for my life. "You're dripping on my head, Ned," I told him.

"I can't help it," Sam said. "Paint falls through the holes."

"I don't mind," I said. "I was just letting you know. Check out how much got on me."

When he looked down I snatched his roller.

"I'm doing two legs at once," I said.

Sam yanked it out of my hand and across my shirt.

"Give me a break, Jake," I said. "The top is flat. Flat is easy."

"Fine, I'll do the top plus one leg," Sam said. "But I'm still going to win, Flynn."

"We'll see, Flea."

The faster we rolled the funnier we got. "I'm ten seconds from winning," I said.

Then I stopped short. "Where's Julia?"

Sam dropped his roller and yelled, "Julia!"

"I white ear," she said.

She was behind us, sitting in Wet Chair Number One.

Sam picked her up fast. "Julia! You were supposed to stay on the steps," he said.

The backs of Julia's legs, arms, and clothes had the same black diamond pattern of the chair.

I rubbed her elbow with spit. "It just smears," I said.

"Your hands are full of paint," Sam said.

Julia let out a cry so big, it echoed. That is, I thought it echoed. The second scream turned out to be Mrs. Alswang. I was right when I said she would go nuts when she saw the chairs.

She ran down the steps and snatched Julia from Sam.

"Don't worry, Mom," Sam said. "She's fine."

Mrs. Alswang was furious. "What are you doing?" she said.

"Pannin," Julia said. "I pannin."

"Look at her hands!" Mrs. Alswang said.

"Sands!" Julia said, and patted her mom's cheeks.

"Her hands and knees!" Mrs. Alswang said.

"Sands and niece," Julia sang. She was proud.

"What were you thinking?" Sam's mom asked.

"We were helping," Sam said.

"My mom says it's too hard for you to take care of two kids," I said.

"She says that?" Mrs. Alswang asked.

"I TOLD Julia to STAY on the step," Sam said. "SHE didn't LISTEN."

"She's a baby," Mrs. Alswang said.

"We never knew this paint is unwashable," I said.

"We were surprising Dad," Sam said.

"I am surprised that you didn't ask permission," his mom said.

"I didn't think of it," Sam said.

"We're sorry," I said.

"On the good side, the chairs turned out great," Sam said.

"Except the one Julia sat on," I said. "It has baby butt prints."

"How am I going to get this paint off her?" Mrs. Alswang asked.

"It'll wear off by the time she gets married," I said.

"That is not funny, Adam," she said.

"It was funny when Dad said it," Sam told her.

"I'll clean up Julia," his mom said. "You clean up the mess."

Sam shouted, "Look out for the Paintmobile!"

Too late.

Mrs. Alswang kicked off her sandal. She looked like she was wearing a black sock.

"Lucky we used a drop cloth, right, Mom?" Sam said.

"That drop cloth is a sheet," she said. "It used to match the guest room."

"Guests won't mind a little paint," Sam said.

"Don't worry about your shoe, Mrs. Alswang," I said. "We'll paint the other one black so they'll match again."

"Please don't," she said. "Just mop up that puddle of paint. And Sam, do not come in the house until all the paint is off your hands and feet."

"I will too," I said.

"Adam," she said, "you are going home."

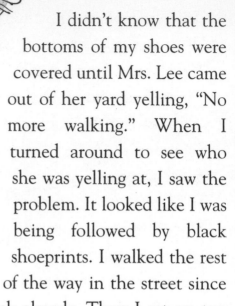

I didn't know that the bottoms of my shoes were covered until Mrs. Lee came out of her yard yelling, "No more walking." When I turned around to see who she was yelling at, I saw the problem. It looked like I was being followed by black shoeprints. I walked the rest of the way in the street since it's black already. Then I sat on top of the corner mailbox and waited for my dad to come walking home.

"Hello, Sport," he said.

"Hello, Dad," I said.

"What happened to your clothes?" he asked. "And your hair?"

"I need a talk," I said.

"Why?"

"Using my head didn't help," I said. "It was totally unpredictable."

"Give me the play-by-play," he said.

When I finished all he said was "Big day."

"Will you still take us to the Big Stink?"

"I'm a man of my word," he said.

I started to give him a hug but he stepped back. "Just thinking of my suit jacket," he said.

Then he asked the usual question.

"I learned not to mix babies and paint," I said.

"I learned a similar thing when I was around your age," he said. "It involved my little brother and maple syrup."

"Mom's going to be mad," I said.

"I think that's likely," my dad said.

"Can you remind her about the ways of boys?" I said.

When we got home my mom was on the phone with Mrs. Alswang. I took the L.O.D. out of my pocket and smoothed it out.

Then I wrote:

13. NO paint.

14. NO letting babies near paint. Or syrup.

"I'll go sit in the basement so I won't stain," I said.

# 12

# LIFESAVERS

Sam and I were biking down Capitol Hill. Thanks to gravity it's no pedaling needed. I had my feet on the handlebars for extra control. "Count down," I yelled to Sam.

"Nine days until the Big Stink-a-dink-a-doo," he screamed.

"Look out!" I screamed.

To miss hitting a tourist I steered onto the grass in front of the National Gallery of Art. Then I somersaulted off my bike.

"Oh! Oh! Ay-yi-yi!" the lady said.

Sam dropped his bike next to mine. "Good reaction, Jackson," he said.

"I'm slick, Toothpick."

"Jackson?" the lady said. "Are you hurt?"

She had an accent. It could be French or German.

"I'm fine," I said. "Believe me."

She looked at my elbow.

"It's just a scrape," I told her. "Don't worry. It happens all the time."

"Okay," she said. "Bye, Jackson. Bye, Toothpick."

We sat on the lawn picking the red pieces out of the Franken Berry cereal from my pocket.

"What are those things in the fountain?" I asked.

We left our bikes and crossed the street. "Baby ducks!" Sam said. "Four of them!"

"Zero parent ducks," I said.

"They're probably orphans," Sam said.

"Of course they are," I said. "If they had a mother she would be here."

"Are ducks born with fish-catching instinct?" Sam asked.

"Maybe," I said. "But they'll never catch them in this fountain."

"They're going to starve," Sam said.

I pointed. "One just got pounded with water."

"They could drown," Sam said.

"Not with us here to save them," I told him.

"What are we doing?" Sam asked.

"You catch one. I catch one. We'll carry them to the Potomac River," I said. "Then we'll come back for the other two."

"That will work," he said.

"This is a great opportunity for B.I.G. F.A.R.T.S.S.," I said. "We are performing an outstandingly heroic job."

"When we tell your dad that we rescued these infant ducks, he will flip," Sam said. "He'll know we are responsible boys who will behave in New York City."

Sam hates it when I stand on his shoulders but it was the only way to reach into the fountain. The fountain sides were almost as tall as me.

I hung on to the inside edge and pulled. "Push my feet up," I screamed.

My stomach didn't slide easily.

I swung my leg around. "I'm riding this ledge like a horse," I said. "All you have to do is grab my hands and walk up the wall."

"This is killing my legs," Sam said. "And my stomach. And my arms. And my butt."

"Hurry up," I said. "Before my arms pop their sockets."

Sam caught his foot on top. I grabbed the edge of his shorts.

"I'm pulling as hard as I can," I said.

Too hard, it turned out. Sam shot forward and knocked me into the water.

Since I had a death grip on his pants he automatically followed.

The next thing I knew I was drenched and holding empty shorts.

"Do not panic," Sam screamed. "I went to Junior Lifeguards!"

He threw his arm around my neck. "Don't fight me, Melonhead. I know what I'm doing!" he screamed. "Relax. I'm saving you."

It's hard to be heard when someone keeps bobbing your head underwater. "Bup we ca tand!" I shouted. "Dand I cans wim."

"No talking. Save your strength!" Sam shouted.

I pulled my knees forward and stood up. "It's not that deep," I said.

"Oh," Sam said.

"Look under!" I said.

"Under where?" Sam asked.

I waved his wet shorts in the air. Sam laughed. "Who lost their pants?"

Then he realized. "I didn't feel them come off," he said. "Give them to me!"

I tossed them at him. "You have snake hips," I said.

He was trying to put them on when he slipped under the pouring fountain.

"Grab my hand," I shouted.

Before he could, I landed on my butt. Who knew the bottom was covered with algae? Not me.

A voice above us yelled, "Hold on, boys."

It came from a man in a light blue suit. He was standing on the fountain ledge, throwing his jacket behind him.

He belly flopped. We tried to help. Then we were all sliding all over the place.

"Don't worry," I said. "We're not drowning. We're saving ducks."

"From what?" the man said.

I was going to answer when I got distracted by looking up. "We're more popular than the cherry blossoms," I said.

The only person we knew in the crowd was the lady tourist. "Toothpick," she yelled. "Jackson! You're hurt?"

"We're on a search-and-rescue mission," I yelled, and threw myself under the pounding water. Sam's cargo shorts had escaped again and were rolling around like they were in a washing machine.

"Got them," I said, and threw them at Sam. The wet man had his arms over his head so he could hold on to the ledge. His red tie was leaking onto his white shirt.

"Thanks for trying to save us, mister," I said.

Sam pulled up his shorts as high as they could go. Then he waded over to the man. "Sir, people are staring at your head," he whispered.

You know Two-Face in the Batman comics? This guy was Two-Hair. On one side his hair was so long it touched his shoulder. The other side was super-short. On top was no hair at all.

The man turned as pink as his shirt. He swooped up the long side and smoothed it across his head to the short side.

"Hey," I said. "You don't look bald anymore."

People started clapping. At first I thought it was for his trick hair. Then I decided it was for us. I took a bow.

People were yelling but we couldn't hear over the beeping car horns. That's how come we missed the other honking.

I was dive-bombed. A big, flapping duck grabbed a beakful of shirt and a big pinch of skin. I saved myself by going underwater and thrashing around. When I came up for air Sam was under quack attack.

"They're not orphans," I said.

The mother duck charged me again.

"We're your friends," I told her.

I reached in my pocket and threw a handful of tan squish at her. "Go get it, girl," I yelled. "It's Franken Mush. You'll love it."

"Uh-oh," Sam said. "Look behind you." He looked horrified.

"Is it the father duck?" I screamed.

"No," Sam said.

"Put your hands up!" a voice said.

It was a policewoman.

The man with the cool hair picked me up by my waist and passed me up to her. If somebody surprised you like that, you'd kick too.

The officer grabbed my hands and pulled me up and out.

"Give me the other one," she told the man.

Sam was under the falling water, hiding from the mother duck. The unbald man dragged him out and boosted him up. The officer sat him next to me on the ledge. Her badge said DURBIN.

Officer Durbin yelled at the guy the whole time she was pulling him out. "I have seen some irresponsible people before but this beats everything. You took your kids swimming in a public fountain! Bare-bottomed, no less."

"I was not naked!" Sam said.

"I didn't take them swimming," the man said. "They went in after the ducks."

"You let them chase defenseless ducklings?" she said. "What kind of parent does that?"

"I'm not a parent!" the man yelled. "I don't know these kids."

"And yet you took them into a fountain?" she said.

"We took ourselves in," I said. "We were rescuing ducks. He was rescuing us."

"Only it turned out nobody needed to be saved," Sam said.

"He ruined his suit to save us," I said.

"You did?" Officer Durbin said.

"You don't know how much I wish I didn't," the man said.

"I didn't realize you were being a good citizen," she said. "My apologies."

I leaned over and whispered, "Hair."

The guy gave it the old swoop-over. He looked like he was embarrassed. "At least you kept your pants," Sam told him.

The man dropped down to the ground and took off.

Officer Durbin walked us back to our bikes. "I was ten years old once," she said.

"Once long ago," Sam said.

"Not THAT long ago," she said. "And I am all for saving animals. But if you EVER swim, WADE, or THINK about stepping in a public fountain again, I'll take you down to the station and call your parents."

"Thank you for not calling this time," I said.

"His mom is the panicking type," Sam told her.

Riding home with the wind on the wet was like having built-in air-conditioning. By the time we got to my house we were completely dry.

My mom gave us Popsicles. "You boys make me proud," she said.

"We do?" I asked.

She smiled. "I know it wasn't easy, but isn't it worth it? Four hours of playing around and your clothes are still tidy. No rips. No stains. Except for the paint in your hair, you look cleaner than you have all summer."

# 13
## UH-OH

My dad got home in time for banana pudding.

"Daddy-O-Dad," I said. "The big day is coming soon. Let's leave at five a.m.!"

"We'd better leave at four-thirty," he said. "The Big Stink waits for no man."

"Or boys," I said.

My dad leaned over my mom's chair and kissed her head. "How goes the garden?"

"If the ladybugs would get to work it would be great," she said. "How was your day?"

"Our meeting at the Newseum went so well, we finished early," he said.

"I hope you had time for a nice lunch," she said.

"I thought I would but traffic was stalled up and down Constitution Avenue," he said. "I couldn't catch a cab. I ended up walking fourteen blocks back to the office."

"Maybe the president's motorcade was in the neighborhood," my mom said.

"Maybe," he said. "Let's take a look at your prizewinning garden before supper."

"Your phone is ringing," I said.

"It's the office," he said. "I'll make it quick."

He did.

"That was Roxanne Lopez," he said. "She said she sent me something from YouTube and I have to drop everything and look."

"Is this bad news?" my mom asked.

"No," he said. "She said it's the funniest thing she's seen in months."

"Let's look!" I said.

"Let's look at the garden first," he said.

"The garden will always be there," I said.

"So will the video," my dad said. "The Internet lasts forever."

"Please?" I asked.

"Go ahead," my mom said. "Adam was so responsible today, I'll turn my time slot over to him."

My dad opened his laptop and clicked on Mrs. Lopez's message. "It's called 'DC Ducklings,'" he said.

My stomach hit my feet.

"Forget it," I said. "I changed my mind. Who cares about seeing ducks? Not me."

My dad hit Play.

"They're so cute," my mom said.

"But not funny," I said. "Let's go outside, right now. We can have a night of looking at flowers and family talking. Mom loves those."

"Shhh!" my mom said.

"This is boring," I said, "I'm going outside."

"Hold your horses, Sport," my dad said.

My feeling was desperate.

"Screen time rots your brain," I said. "Believe me. If you don't, ask Sam's mom. Turn it off before it's too late."

It already was. I was flopping around in the fountain, right before my own eyes. Sam's underpants were showing. Baby ducks were squawking. The suit man was belly flopping.

"Poor guy!" My mom laughed. "Look at his hair!"

"This is hilarious," my dad said.

"Whew," I said. "I was afraid you'd be mad."

My mom stared at the screen. "Is that you, Adam?" she said.

"Is that Sam?" my dad said.

"You are IN a FOUNTAIN!" my mom said.

"Why did you go in a fountain?" my dad asked.

"Nobody ever told me I couldn't go in fountains," I said. "How could I know?"

"You could have drowned. Or been bitten by a duck. Or arrested. I can't bear to think how many eye infections you caught."

"This is a fowl attack!" my dad said. "Look at the mother duck going after you, Sport!"

"Why would she do that? They're kids," my mom said. "And Adam, how deep is that fountain?"

"It wasn't over our heads," I said. "See, there's Sam, standing up."

"And falling down," my dad said.

"It's the police!" my mom said. "You did get arrested!"

"Stop breathing, Mom," I said. "I mean slow down! I didn't get arrested."

Her breaths got even faster.

"Sport," my dad said. "Did you consider the consequences before you jumped in?"

"No," I said. "Because we didn't jump. We fell. There was zero danger."

"Aunt Cindy says that the situations you get into are signs of your intelligence," my mom said. "I am clinging to that idea."

I pulled out the damp List of Doom.

She wrote:

15. NO fountains.

16. NO duck rescues.

# 14
## S-U-R-P-R-I-S-E

I have the forgiving type of mom. She is not the forgetting type.

"Darling boy," she said. "There's a new deal today. You may go out, but only to Parks and Rec."

"Without fenceball, it's boring," I said.

"I like boring," she said. "I like peace, quiet, and knowing that my son is not swimming with ducks and without lifeguards."

"Okay," I said. Even though we had the setback, we were still on the B.I.G.F.A.R.T.S.S. program. It includes no complaining.

"Also, Mrs. Hackett's yard looks like a postcard.

To have any hope of winning I need to work all day, every day. I need cooperation."

Even though it wasn't Sam's consequence, he went with me to Parks & Rec.

"What did your parents say?" I asked.

"That good intentions are not the same as good ideas," Sam said. "I had to sit in my room and think about my judgment."

"Did you?"

"Mostly I thought your dad might not take us to New York."

"He will," I said. "He promised."

"I also read," Sam said. "Did you know the red on the Big Stink is made out of about a million practically microscopic flowers that are so close they blend together? The coolest part is it sucks the lives out of other plants."

"They should name it the titan vampirum," I said.

"I wonder what the Big Stink is sucking the life out of right now," he said.

"When they're in captivity they feed off of fertilizer and minerals," I told him.

"The botanical garden is probably against plant murder," Sam said.

We were climbing over the preschool playground fence when Sam said, "Triple Red Alert! Justin's here."

I turned around mid-fence.

"Hey," Justin said.

"Hey," Sam said back. Then he poked my back. That was code for *You are making it worse*.

"Hey," I said.

"I saw you at Jimmy T's," Justin said.

"I'm Sam," Sam said. "He's Melonhead."

"I know," Justin said to me. "I'm Justin."

"Like Justin time?" I said. Then I was embarrassed.

"I've never heard that before," Justin said.

"Really?" I asked.

"No," he said. "Do you know anybody here who plays basketball?"

"We play basketball," Sam said.

He was ignoring my supersonic brain waves.

"Are you any good?" Justin said.

"No," I said.

"Me either," he said. "Want to play H-O-R-S-E? Sam, go first."

Sam grabbed the ball.

"You can go second," I said.

Even though Parks & Rec basketballs are short on bounce, I got H on the first try. That was a relief. Sam and Justin didn't make baskets. Then Justin got four in a row. "Skunked you!" he said, and bounced the ball around our legs. "How about double or nothing? The loser buys Cokes at Jimmy T's."

"I'm broke," Sam said.

"I have a quarter," I said.

"Chump change," Justin said. "But that's okay. Win or lose, I'll pay."

"Really?" I asked.

"I have a job," he said.

"What is it?" Sam asked.

Justin mumbled, "I babysit."

"We used to," I said. "We got fired for letting the baby get soaked in paint."

"Anybody would get fired for that," Justin said.

We played four more games. The furthest I got was H-O-R-S. Sam only got to R. Justin won.

At Jimmy T's, we sat at the counter.

"Quit spinning," Mrs. T said. "You're going to twirl yourself onto the floor again."

"Limeade or Cherry Smash?" Justin said. "I can't decide."

"I'm the King of Combos," I said. "Today I'm having half Coke, half grape soda."

"I'll try that," Justin said.

Sam got chocolate milk, extra syrup.

"Want to hang out tomorrow?" I asked.

"Sure," Justin said. "Where do you live?"

When I told him he said, "I'll come around one o' clock."

My mom didn't notice that I was ten minutes late.

"Sit on the flagstone while I tend the nasturtiums," she said. "Tell me about your day."

"We met up with a guy named Justin," I said. "I used to think he was mean. He's not. He's the best teenager I ever met."

I told about H-O-R-S-E and Jimmy T's. "Oops," I said. "I forgot I was supposed to stay on the playground."

"That's okay," my mom said.

"You are in a great mood," I said.

"I got a lot done today," she said. "Now I'm impatiently waiting for the impatiens to grow."

That was a joke.

"If I were a justice I'd vote for you," I said.

She smiled. "Tell me more about your new friend."

"Even though he's fifteen we have identical interests," I said. "I like inventing. He likes inventing. I like science. He likes science. I collect the red wax that comes on cheese. He used to collect the red wax that comes on cheese. When it got bigger than a kickball he sold it to his cousin for six bucks. He's jealous that Sam and I will be smelling the Big Stink in person."

"Sam likes him?" my mom said.

"Sure," I said. "You will too. We're hanging out tomorrow after I get off from Mrs. Wilkins."

"Sounds fun," she said.

I could have gone into shock. "Don't you want to meet him first to make sure he doesn't get too close to the edge at the Metro and all that stuff?"

"Of course I do," she said. "You can't go running off with careless strangers."

# 15

# RESCUE NUMBER TWO

*I* knocked on Mrs. Wilkins's door at 7:40 a.m. I waited. I knocked again. No answer. I knocked with the knocker and my fist. After eight nonstop minutes I got nervous because what if something had happened?

I pushed my lips inside the mail slot. "Mrs. Wilkins! It's me, Melonhead. I'm ready to work."

Nothing.

"Are you okay?!" I yelled. No answer.

I screamed. "Are your hips busted? Can you answer?"

When she didn't, I knew things were terrible.

"Hold on," I hollered. "I'm getting help! If your bones are broken, don't move."

I learned that from TV.

I ran down Fourth Street, crossed Pennsylvania Avenue, and cut through Garfield Park so fast my lungs stabbed. I didn't stop until I was in the E Street Police Station.

I could barely breathe. "Officer Bazemore! Help! It's an emergency."

"Slow down, Melonhead," she said. "Breathe."

I know her from the time I almost caused a car crash by walking backwards.

"Something happened to Mrs. Wilkins," I said.

"What?" she asked.

"I don't know," I said. "But she's old as can be and she isn't answering the door."

"Maybe she's asleep," Officer Bazemore said.

"Impossible," I said. "She doesn't sleep. She says a cat walking on snow would wake her up."

"Could she be on vacation?" Officer Bazemore asked. "Out for a walk, or at Eastern Market? The farmers put out the best produce early."

"Mrs. Wilkins doesn't visit. She doesn't walk. Food comes to her, the same as I do. She doesn't go farther than her yard unless she's going to the doctor's, and they're not open yet. I'm scared." That part was private. I didn't mean to admit it. "This is a true emergency. Believe me."

"What's the address?" she asked.

"I don't know."

Officer Bazemore had to stay at the station. Officer Dicutus and Officer Lelong got the case.

"Hop in the back of the cruiser," Officer Lelong said. "We need you to show us where Mrs. Wilkins lives."

Even though the windows were up, the siren was loud. "I'm riding in a cage," I yelled.

"Sorry about that," Officer Dicutus said. "The screen doesn't open."

"I'm not sorry," I said. "I've always wanted to ride in the arrested people's space."

"Don't like it too much," he said.

"I never knew police car backseats are made of hard plastic," I said. "They feel exactly like uncomfortable chairs."

"Get your lips off that screen," Officer Lelong said.

"Turn here," I said.

We did and guess who was standing on the corner? Ashley and her mom, that's who. "Do the prisoner windows go down?" I asked.

They don't. I waved with both hands.

"Which house?" Officer Dicutus asked.

"The redbrick one with the birdbath," I said.

We double-parked. Officer Lelong flipped off the siren. They raced to the door. I felt bad for enjoying the police car ride when Mrs. Wilkins was hurt. Or tied up by robbers. I hadn't thought of that before.

Officer Dicutus banged the door knocker.

"She can't answer," I said.

Officer Lelong went back to the car and got on the speaker. "Mrs. Wilkins, this is the DCPD. Are you able to come to the door?"

Nothing.

Officer Lelong said it again.

"You'll have to kick down the door," I said.

That's when the front door flew open. There was Mrs. Wilkins. She had on a pink bathrobe and no shoes. Her chin was hanging down.

"The robbers knocked out your teeth!" I screamed. "Good thing I got the law."

"Mrs. Wilkins?" Officer Lelong said.

"Since when is it illegal to take a shower?" Mrs. Wilkins said. It came out whistley because of her having no teeth.

"This young man thought you were in trouble," Officer Dicutus said.

"Why?" Mrs. Wilkins asked.

"You didn't answer your door," I said. "I thought your hips finally busted."

"I was asleep," she said.

I couldn't believe it.

"But you don't sleep," I said. "You told me."

"I don't sleep much," she said. "And never with my hearing aid," she told the officers.

"I'm glad you're well," Officer Dicutus said. "We're sorry we disturbed you."

Mrs. Wilkins gave me the stare of dread. "You got the police?" she asked.

"I didn't want you to turn up dead," I said.

When my mom saw me running up our block, she raced to me in a speed-breathing panic. "What happened? Ashley said you got arrested. I've been calling the police. You scared me to death."

"Why would I be arrested?" I said.

"Ashley didn't know. She said they took you away in a squad car," my mom told me.

"I was taking them," I said. "I almost saved Mrs. Wilkins's life."

My mom looked horrified. "You were too late?"

"Too early," I said. "She wasn't awake yet."

"Thank goodness Winnie is okay," my mom said.

"Today's police said I was responsible," I told her. "I think Mrs. Wilkins was glad I came to the rescue."

"Why?" my mom asked.

"She said, 'I see how you got your nickname.' Then she gave me the day off."

"How about that?" my mom said.

"That means I'm done," I said. "This was my third time."

"Today doesn't count," my mom said.

# 16
# THE GREATEST DAY

Justin came over after lunch.

"Lovely to meet you," my mom said.

"Thanks," he said.

"What are you boys doing this afternoon?" she asked.

Supersonic brain wave to Mom: DON'T ASK BABYISH QUESTIONS.

"We're knocking around," Justin said. "Sam's meeting us at Eastern Market."

"Adam," my mom said. "Treat yourself and your friends to something fun."

She gave me a five-dollar bill.

"You are not the type of mother who gives away free money," I said.

"It looks like I am today," she said. "Have fun doing guy things."

On the way I told Justin how I almost saved Mrs. Wilkins.

"Man," he said. "I'm impressed. Lots of kids your age would stand there wondering what to do."

I liked that.

Sam had been waiting for seventeen minutes.

"It's my mom's fault, Walt," I said. "She kept talking."

"No biggie, Piggie," Sam said.

I waved my money in front of his eyes.

"Donuts!" Sam said.

"Atomic Fireballs last longer," I told him.

"I say we buy the biggest watermelon we can find and eat the whole thing," Justin said.

Why didn't I think of that?

Mrs. Calamaris gave us an ice-cold deal. It was almost as heavy as Julia. We took turns carrying it to Seward Square Park.

"It's a backbreaker," Justin said.

I was glad he'd said it. I didn't want to seem weak. "I'm getting Gumby arms," I said.

At the park Justin told me, "Drop it."

"Drop it?"

"Yeah," he said. "Let go. Splat."

It was like slow motion. The watermelon crashed on the cement, bounced and busted in pieces.

"Wow," Sam said.

"I wish I could do it again," I said.

Justin gave me the first chunk. "Melon for Melon," he said.

He and Sam picked the next biggest pieces off the sidewalk.

"Seed-spitting contest!" I called.

You win some of those and you lose some of those.

When the only thing left was rind, we lay on our backs and looked at the sky. I told about a project I'm planning to make one day.

"You should do it soon," Justin said.

Before we left, we clawed holes in the dirt and planted watermelon seeds. "How long before this park will be a patch?" I asked.

"Depends on rain," Justin said.

On the way home Sam said, "I can't believe a teenager wants to be our friend."

"Believe it," I said.

# 17

# THE SHRUNKEN HEADS

I got to Mrs. Wilkins's at ten o'clock this morning.

"Hey!" I said. "Dr. Bowers fixed your teeth! They look exactly like before."

"It's too hot to work in the attic today," she said.

"Okay," I said. "See you tomorrow."

"I'll see you today and tomorrow," she said. "Today we'll work in the backyard."

I wanted to say, "This is my last day." But what I said was "I love your backyard."

"You do?" she asked.

"Doesn't everybody?"

"I've had a few complaints," she said.

"Pop says some people wouldn't recognize a masterpiece if it was in their nose," I said. "This is a top place in Washington."

Mrs. Wilkins stayed on the porch, sitting in her green metal chair and yelling down directions. "I'm making sure you don't go yanking up valuable plants," she said.

"I won't," I said.

She snorted. "Get a bag of gravel out of the shed. It's on a shelf next to things that look like shrunken heads. Bring those too."

"Are they really shrunken heads?" I asked.

She didn't answer.

Inside the shed was a junk heap but the heads were easy to spot. They looked like scrunched-up dead wads with interesting hairy parts.

I carried them up to the porch. "Not very head-like," I said.

"Get those bowls on the windowsill," she said. "Put a handful of gravel in each one."

She added the heads.

"Drag the hose up here," she said. "They're thirsty."

For the first time, I felt sorry for Mrs. Wilkins. "Whatever these are, they're dead," I told her.

"Oh, you're the boss now?" she said.

At least it doesn't take much time to water dead stuff.

"Now it's time to dig up the volunteers," she said.

"People are buried in this yard?" I asked.

"Only the ones I didn't like," she said. Then she laughed. "When seeds fall and plant themselves they're called volunteers. Start with the *Alocasia odora*."

"Which one is it?"

"The strange-looking one," she said.

"They're all strange-looking," I said.

"It's that short one," she said. "Some people call it elephant ear."

"It looks like a mushroom wearing a hood," I said.

"It needs a little sun and a little shade," she said. "Plant it where it can spread out."

"There isn't a place," I said. "Your yard is taken up."

"There's a spot by the basement steps," she said. "First, grab some Zoo Doo from the shed."

I laughed like thirty hyenas. "I don't know what Zoo Doo is, but it's the worst name I ever heard," I said. "People probably think it's poop from the zoo."

"People are right," she said. "The zoo recycles it."

"You're joking," I said.

"It's the best fertilizer in the world," she said.

"What kind of poop is it?" I asked. "Iguana poop? Panda poop? I bet alligator poop is the hardest to collect."

Then I had a brain flash. "There's a job called poop collector?" I asked.

"Stop hooting," Mrs. Wilkins said. "This Zoo Doo comes from alpacas."

"Where do you get alpaca poop?" I said.

"They deliver," she said.

"The alpacas?"

"The garden store," she said.

"May I have alpaca poop for my mom?" I asked. "It could help her win the contest."

"Help yourself," she said. "But watch where you're stepping."

"I'm walking on stones," I said.

"You're stomping on mountain turtles," she said.

I jumped. "I didn't know," I said. "I'm sorry."

Their shells looked odd but they weren't cracked. Thinking that I almost squashed a turtle made me feel terrible.

"They're not animals," she said. "They're rare bulbs from China. You bury half. The other half sits on the ground, looking like a turtle. They send out vines with heart-shaped leaves and flowers."

"They shouldn't call them turtles. That scares people."

"So call them *Stephania rotundifolia*," she said.

"I don't see their vines," I said.

"I don't expect any," she said. "The other plants are blocking the sun."

I dug and planted for two hours. "Did you ever think about getting rid of some plants?" I asked.

"I did not," she said. "And you may not think it either. My husband grew them from the seeds he sent back from all over the world. After bugs and family, plants were what he loved best. You would have me throw them away?"

"No," I said. "They're great. But you're out of space and I'm out of ideas."

"Fine, Mr. Knows Everything," she said. "We'll stop. Put the shovel in the shed and come up and get a bag for the alpaca poop. Unless you want to carry it in your pockets."

On my way up the steps I said, "I was only supposed to work for three days."

She didn't answer.

In a louder voice I said, "Mrs. Wilkins, I was only— Look! The shrunken heads turned into little bushes. They're alive."

"Of course they are," she said. "What would I want with dead plants?"

"How did you make them do that?" I asked.

"You did," she said. "When you watered them."

"You traded them while I was working," I said.

"Suit yourself," she said.

"I'm right, aren't I?"

"I thought you were in a hurry," she said.

"I'm not," I said. "I'm curious."

"They're part of the lycopod family," she said. When they get water they grow. When they can't, they fold up into tight balls and wait. They're called resurrection plants because they look dead and come back to life."

"How long can they last between drinks?" I asked.

"I've had these for at least fifteen years. I don't know how old they were when Mr. Wilkins got them," she said.

"Where did he find them?" I asked.

I'm not sure," she said. "Probably El Salvador or Mexico or Arizona."

I picked one up. "These are the second-best plants ever made."

"Will your mom win the garden contest?" Mrs. Wilkins asked.

"I hope so," I said.

"See you Wednesday," she said.

I wanted to tell her, "You know, you're not the only B.I.G.F.A.R.T.S.S. expert around here," but I don't think she is much of a joker.

# 18

# DIVA DELIVERY

It was my idea to have a water-balloon fight on top of our watermelon patch. "The water cools us, rolls off us, and gets instantly recycled," I said. "Thanks to us for saving the planet."

"Now that we're watered, I feel like a cookie," Justin said.

"I feel like a boy," I said.

"Good one, dude."

"We know the Baking Divas," Sam said.

"Do you know the pretty girl with light brown hair who works on Saturdays?" he asked.

"That's Julianne Meany," Sam said.

"She babysat for me," I said. "When I was a kid, I mean."

"What's she like?" Justin asked.

"She's nice," I said. "Once she found a fox skull."

"Was she grossed out?" Justin asked.

"She was happy," Sam said. "She took it home."

"That's my kind of girl," Justin said.

I didn't know what to say about that.

When we got to the Divas, Aunt Frankie was loading the cake case. "You're right on time for Downtown Brownies," she said.

"This is our friend Justin," I said.

"You're part of the Double Date family," Aunt Frankie said.

"No, ma'am," he said. "I'm a Richardson."

She laughed. "I know families by what they order. Your mom is a Double Date Cake regular."

"Is Jonique here?" I asked.

"That child was supposed to do a delivery for me but ever since she's been going to math camp, numbers are all she can think about," Aunt Frankie said.

"We deliver," I said.

"All right," she said. "Pick your pay."

"A Monumental cookie for me," I said.

"Would you like the Capitol, the Washington Monument, or the Lincoln Memorial?" she asked. "Thomas Jefferson sold out."

I got the Capitol. It's the biggest.

"I'd like a Sweet Jonique," Justin said.

"How about you, Sam?"

"A Smart Blondie, please."

"Where are we going?" Justin asked.

"To Mrs. Wilkins's house on Fourth Street, N.E.," Aunt Frankie said. "I'll get the house number."

"I know which house it is," I said.

"She's a friend of yours?" Aunt Frankie asked.

"I'm not sure," I said. "I'm her helper."

"You have a job?" Justin said.

"Yes, but I don't get paid," I said.

Aunt Frankie packed a Half-a-Pound Cake in a white box and added a free Q.T. Bar. "Mrs. Wilkins is a good customer," she said.

Then she said, "You know my rules. If a customer says their baked goods arrived in pieces, your delivery days are over. And remember, when you work for me, you are an ambassador for the shop."

"We'll treat this cake like it's a baby," I said.

"Oh no you won't," she laughed. "I don't want it to arrive covered with paint."

I don't know how she heard about that.

When I introduced Justin to Mrs. Wilkins she said, "You're a tall boy."

"Like my dad," he said.

"Good for you both," she said. "Come in and change my lightbulb."

It turned out to be four lightbulbs.

"Can I show them the shrunken heads?" I asked.

"Knock yourself out," she said.

It was a fast look.

"I'm going to a party at seven o'clock," Justin told Mrs. Wilkins.

"Then go," she said.

I left with him.

"She's nicer than she seems," I said.

"I hope so," he said.

At two in the morning I woke up with a brain flash. I crept into my mom's workroom and shined my flashlight around in the closet. A roll of Mazel Tov on Your Bar Mitzvah wrapping paper fell on my head. That caused a chain reaction. I used Wedding Wishes and Congratulations, Graduate! to stop the avalanche. Then I found a brown envelope. I stuck on all the stamps we had, except I saved a Frank Sinatra for Lucy Rose's collection. The only thing I know about him is that he's dead. You can't be on a stamp until you are.

I wrote "Mr. Claude Pinot" near the top and the address underneath. The letters came out lumpy. It's hard to be neat when your chin is holding a flashlight.

Then I ran to the corner, dropped it in the

mailbox, and raced back to bed. Luckily, I fell asleep in seconds. You don't want to be tired when Mrs. Wilkins is your boss. Believe me.

# 19

## SUPPLIES

Sam and I were studying the Big Stink when Justin showed up.

"Let's do it," he said.

"Do what?" Sam asked.

"Melonhead's project. He'll show us how to make it. I'll buy the supplies," Justin said.

"Take the deal, Banana Peel," Sam said.

"Let's go to Chateau Animaux, Joe," I said.

"Whatever you say, Clay," Justin said.

For speed we went by skateboard.

"Sam," Justin said, "why did you paint yours black?"

"My mom did it," Sam said.

The Chateau Animaux fish seller knows her tubing. "Hard or flexible?" she asked.

"Hard," I said. "Also, we need an aquarium pump."

"Next stop?" Justin asked.

"Frager's Hardware store," I said.

I asked for the cheapest outside faucet, a plastic bucket, and a can of fast-drying putty.

"Look out back," Mr. Weintraub said. "Faucets are fifty percent off."

"I'll show them," a girl said.

She turned to Justin. "I'm Amy. I've seen you around."

"I'm Justin," he said. "You look familiar."

Amy never notices Sam and me. But she acted like Justin was the best thing since snakes.

"I think I've seen you at the Lavins' house," she said. "I babysit Alex and Isabelle."

"That's probably it," he said. "I'm friends with Caroline and Ellie."

"Come on," Sam said. "Let's find the faucet."

When we came back Amy was still gabbing. "That's so funny, my brother went to Capitol Hill Day School too!" she said.

"What's funny about that?" Sam said.

Nothing, that's what.

"Where are the plastic buckets?" I asked.

Amy pointed and kept talking to Justin.

"Excuse me," I said. "Do you have any super-strange plants?"

"Strictas. They live on air," she said. "No dirt. No pot. No nothing. Just soak them once a week. They're next to pansies."

Sam and I hauled everything to the counter.

I gave Amy two dollars for the stricta. Justin paid for the rest. He must make a lot because the supplies cost a ton, believe me. "We have to go," Justin said. "I need to be someplace by five-thirty."

I bet he had a babysitting job but was embarrassed to say it.

On the way back Sam asked Justin, "Do you want to get a date with her?"

"No," Justin said.

"How come?" I asked.

"She wasn't nice to my friends," Justin said.

When I got home I told my mom, "Have you noticed that Sam and I haven't gotten in any situations for two days?"

"I have," she said. "Congratulations."

"Three cheers for B.I.G.F.A.R.T.S.S.," I said. My mom rolled her eyes.

# 20
## FED UP

This morning, when Mrs. Wilkins opened her door, I held out my hand.

"I hope you are not expecting to be paid, mister."

"Nope," I said. "I bought you something."

"You did?" she said. "Why?"

I whipped around my other hand from behind my back.

"Andy used to collect strictas," she said.

"I made it into a pin," I said. "It won't take up yard space and you can wear it when you go to the doctor's."

"Aren't you smart?" she said.

That might have been sarcastic. I didn't ask because she looked like she was going to cry. Probably air plants remind her of her dead husband.

"Thank you," she said.

Now was the time to say that this was my last time coming. Only with the crying look, I couldn't.

"This is the last day," she said.

Relief plus. "Yes," I said.

"The last day you're going to spend in the attic," she said. "If we don't find my albums today I'm giving up."

I nodded.

"Beginning tomorrow we'll be spending our time on the yard," she said.

I stamped up the attic steps and pulled the light string. Then I made a choice. Whether Mrs. Wilkins knows it or not, I quit. "I am done with looking, done with planting, overdone with personal responsibility," I said, quietly.

I piled up all the purple curtains and plopped down in the middle. I felt like I was the guy in the song about purple mountains' majesty. I picked up

a *National Geographic* magazine from 1967.

"Any luck?" she called up.

"No," I yelled.

"Are you looking care-
fully?" she asked. "Al-
bums don't up and walk
away."

"Maybe someone stole them," I said.

I was being sarcastic.

"Maybe not," she said. "So don't go getting the police."

From the purple mountain I could reach a round box. It said "Garfinkle's" on top.

"Makes a good table," I said, to myself.

"Speak up," Mrs. Wilkins said.

"I'll tell you if I find something," I said.

Inside the table box was a hat covered with fake yellow flowers. Underneath was a pink hat. It looked like a Frisbee. The bottom hat was small and black. It had a miniature net on the front. I do not get the point of ladies' hats. I stuffed them back in my table and enjoyed the luxury of being retired.

"Is there a place you haven't checked?" Mrs. Wilkins yelled.

I yelled back, "Nope."

"Well, come on down," she said.

I was in the middle of a story about marsupials but I went.

She looked sad.

"Sorry," I said.

"You tried your hardest," she said. "Thank you."

Two thanks in one day?

"Why do you need them so much?" I asked.

"Well, Mr. Nose in My Business, if you must know, I'm getting my hip replaced."

"With what?" I asked.

"With a fake hip, of course. What do you think they'd put in there? A butter dish?"

"What are fake hips made out of?" I asked.

"Titanium," she said. "It's a metal. After it's been in for a while, new bone grows around it."

"I would like to see that," I said.

"Forget it," she said.

"You'll probably have to go to the hospital to get it," I said.

"I do," she said.

"They should make resurrection hips," I said. "Every time you got wet they would get strong again."

"Invent that and you'll be a millionaire," she said.

"I'll work on it," I said.

I felt like I'd been mean.

"What do albums have to do with your hip?" I asked.

"Molly is coming from Tunisia next month to stay with me after my surgery," she said. "I think she'd like to look at them."

"You mean listen to them," I said.

"Why would I mean that?" she said.

That got me thinking.

"One question," I said. "What exactly is an album?"

"Don't be a nitwit," she said.

"I'm not," I said.

"After all this you didn't know what you were looking for?" she said. Not too nicely.

"Albums are flat, cardboard squares with a slit on one side, right? Madam and Pop have some in their basement," I said. "Inside is a black plastic circle with a little hole in the middle. In the olden days they put them on a player and music came out. Pop calls them records but Madam says they're albums."

Mrs. Wilkins looked at me. "Thick as a box of rocks."

"No," I said. "They're thinner than a centipede."

"Did you see books with photographs pasted in them?"

"They're on top of Franklin's notes," I said.

"Why didn't you bring them to me?" she said.

"You said don't go near that stuff," I said.

"Get them," she said. "Please."

When I did she hugged them.

"These are albums?" I asked.

"Yes," she said.

"If you had said scrapbooks I would have gotten them first try," I said.

"Well, you found them eventually," she said. "That's something."

"Are there any more pictures of you in your airplane?" I asked.

"Let's see," she said.

She opened the book and smiled. "This is my husband," she said.

"He's young," I said.

"He was," she said, and turned the page.

"Where'd he get those monkeys?" I asked.

"Monkeys were all over Africa," she said. "We had one that came to see us for every meal. We tried to keep him from grabbing food but he always outsmarted us."

"What did you do?" I asked.

"Named him Pepe," she said. "Once we decided to call him our pet, I didn't mind having him at the table. He had his own chair  and better manners than my children."

"You were a fun mom," I said.

She had pictures of Pepe outside with his monkey family and inside with his people family.

"He could play catch," she said. "If he got mad he'd put the ball under his arm and climb up high. The game was over."

I pointed at the next one. "There's a toucan on your head," I said.

"I had forgotten all about that toucan," she said.

"How can anybody forget a toucan?" I said.

This time she smiled.

# 21

## EXCELLENT DEMONSTRATION

"This is awesome," Justin said. "The H2O4U IS amazing."

"They'll flip when they find out we made it in twenty minutes," Sam said.

Sam put the H2O4U on the Alswangs' outside table. I covered it with a beach towel. Lucy Rose and Jonique helped Justin line up the chairs.

"Melonhead and I painted those two," Sam said.

"Open the gate. Let in the crowd," Justin said.

My dad was first in line.

"Where's Mom?" I asked.

"She had to see a man about some aphids," my dad said. "She's sad to be missing your top-secret project."

"Attention, everyone, please take a seat and enjoy the show," Lucy Rose said.

Julia waved her finger at my dad. "NOSE IT TOWN." She pulled his pants. "Nose IT TOWN," she said. When he didn't understand, Julia crawled under his chair, pushed her fingers through the diamond-shaped holes, and poked his butt. "Sup yoogo," she yelled. "Painon pans. Painon pans."

"Julia?" my dad asked. "Do you want me to stand up?"

Julia looked at the back of his pants. Then she walked around and looked at the front. "No painon pans?"

"No paint on pants," I said. "The paint is dry."

Julia patted my dad's leg. "Nye spans," she said.

Sam's parents laughed. I think they are over that incident.

This time my dad sat next to Madam. "We're ready to be dazzled," Pop said.

I plugged it into the extension cord.

Then Sam said, "Presenting the H2O4U!"

"Is that the scientific name?" Madam asked.

I pulled off the towel.

"Why, it's a floating faucet!" Madam said.

I waved my hand behind the faucet. "Ladies and gentlemen," I said. "As you can see, the H2O4U is not hooked up to a pipe."

"But water is pouring out anyway, into this bucket," Sam said. "It's H2O4U."

"That's impossible," Jonique said.

"Believe your own eyes," I said.

When no one could guess how it worked Justin pulled out the plug.

The water stopped.

"It looks like a plastic tube with a faucet stuck on top," Sam's mom said.

"I don't get it," Lucy Rose said.

"There's a bowl inside the bucket," I said. "And an aquarium pump in the bowl."

"Rocks are covering the pump," Sam said.

"The tube attaches to the pump," Justin said. "The pump sends water through the tube."

"So why doesn't the water spray out of the back of the faucet?" my dad asked.

"E-Z P-Z," I said. "We put a wad of quick-drying putty inside the faucet. The water gets pumped up the inside tube but it's blocked by the putty. So it makes a U-turn and runs down the outside of the tube."

"And gets sucked back up the inside of the tube," Justin said. "It uses the same water over and over again."

"Since the tube is clear it doesn't show," Sam said. "Plus it makes it look like there's more water than there actually is."

"I see," Sam's mom said. "You weren't fooling around in a public fountain. You were doing research."

That made everybody laugh.

"You should go into the fountain-making business," Mr. Alswang said.

"We can call it Mountains of Fountains," I said.

"Sign us up," Madam said. "We'll buy one."

"I am dumbfounded," my dad said.

"That is not the same as being dumb," Lucy Rose said. "He's just too utterly shocked to talk."

Sam's dad took pictures of us with the fountain turned on and off.

"I am proud and amazed," my dad said. "I can't wait to see what you're going to teach me in New York."

"I have cookies and juice inside," Sam's mom said.

"I've got to get back to the office," my dad told her. "Bring the H2O4U home so Mom can see it."

"Okay," I said.

# 22

# THE FIRST TWO PARTS OF THE THREE-PART DISASTER

Sam and I had a meeting at the library. "We need all the biographies of Odoardo Beccari," Sam told Ms. McKinney.

She looked. "Sorry, boys," she said. "We don't have anything like that. In fact, I never heard of Mr. Beccari."

"Are you kidding?" I said. "You don't know the great botanist who discovered the titan arum? In 1878, in Sumatra, Indonesia?"

"Nope," she said.

"I can't believe that in a huge library like this there aren't any books about him," Sam said.

"Maybe you two boys will have to write one," she said.

She did find some good info on the computer.

When I got home both parents were already there.

"Hello-O, Mom-O," I said. "And hello-O, Dad-O. Why are you home so early?"

"I need to talk to you," he said.

"Is it about my personal responsibility?" I asked.

"It's about MY personal responsibility," he said.

He put his hands on my shoulders and looked at me close-up.

"I'm so, so sorry, Sport," he said. "I can't take you to New York this weekend."

I felt like I was carsick.

"The Big Stink can't wait," I said.

"I know," he said.

"But we have to be in New York in two days."

"I have to go to Florida tonight," he said.

I felt like I could cry.

"This is the Congressman's fault, isn't it?" I said.

"It's not his fault, Sport," my dad said. "It's his job, and mine. Remember when the Congressman sponsored a law to preserve the lands near Crocodile Lake and Ding Darling?"

"The law passed," I said. "The land is safe."

"Some people figured out a way around the law," he said. "They got a permit to pave some swampland. If we don't stop it now, it will be too late."

"The Congressman can go by himself," I said.

"I wish with all my heart that he could," my dad said. "But I'm the one who put together the law. The Congressman won't be able to explain it well enough to get a judge to stop it."

"He should do his own work," I said.

"It's more than one person can do," he said.

"I counted on you," I said. "Sam still is."

"I am so sorry," my dad said.

"You promised," I said. "You said you were a man of your word."

"I know," he said.

"This is your worst day of parenting," I said.

"It feels like that to me, too, Sport," he said. "But I will make it up to you."

"That's impossible," I said. I was going to say I would never believe him again. But I didn't. He was already sadder than I had ever seen him. So was I.

"Can you bring home a crocodile egg from Ding Darling?" I joked.

He smiled. "It would make a lovely gift for Mom."

My mom laughed and hugged us both at the same time.

It's hard to be mad and sad at the same time.

"I'll tell Sam," my dad said.

"He's with Justin at Parks and Rec," I said. "I'll go with you."

"Me too," my mom said.

When Sam saw us he ran over screaming, "Two more days, two more days."

"Sam," my dad said. "I have to break my word. I have a work emergency. I'm sorry."

Sam had the same look he had when that bee stung his nose. Even his eyes looked shocked and hurt.

Justin asked Sam, "Could your dad take you guys?"

"No," Sam said. "You can't run out on brides."

"Only kids," I said to my dad.

"I'm serving butter brickle ice cream in the backyard," my mom said.

"I don't care," I said.

"I do," Justin said.

At home, my mom scooped ice cream. My dad went upstairs to pack. Sam and I were too miserable to talk. My mom was too miserable not to talk. That meant Justin got a tour of our yard. "I packed this corner with Queen Anne's lace and delphinium," she explained.

"Nice," Justin said.

She showed him the barrels of sweet pea flowers

on the porch and the calla lilies, cosmos, zinnias, and marguerites in the flower beds. "I'll bet you are wondering what these sweet pink flowers are called," she said.

I bet he was not.

"I have had enough of this garden," I said. It came out louder and meaner than I expected.

"I like it," Justin said.

"Me too," Sam said, softly.

"I hope you lose," I told my mom.

I left my bowl on the step and walked through the house and out the front door.

Justin and Sam followed me. "You were rude, dude," Justin said. "It's not your mom's fault that you can't go."

"I know," I said.

"Cool off," he said. "Seriously."

"Come back," Sam said. "Your mom is giving us seconds."

"Go without me," I said.

While they were out back my mom came out front.

"Sorry I was rude and deranged," I said.

"I'm glad you're sorry," she said. "You hurt my feelings."

"I never thought Dad would bail out on us," I said.

"Dad didn't think it either," she said. "He REALLY wanted to be with you."

"I do care if you win," I said. "I wish I could take back what I said. I feel like a skunk. A skunk and varmint mixed together."

"A skarmint?" my mom said. Then she said, "I can take you and Sam to New York."

"You'd miss the contest."

"I'll enter next year," she said.

"No, stay here and win," I said.

My dad came out, carrying his suitcase. "Goodbye, Sport," he said. "I love you."

He hugged my mom. "I'll take the Metro to the airport and call when I get to Florida," he said.

"Go, fight, win," she said. "Save swamps."

We sat around.

"I'd better go," Justin said.

"I'll walk you to the door," my mom said.

"The ice cream is turning to butter brickle soup," Sam said.

"Soup is healthy, right?" I said.

Sam tipped the carton up to his mouth. "Nutritious and delicious," he said.

"My turn," I said.

I opened my mouth as wide as I could and filled it up until it was about to overflow.

"Let me help you," Sam said, and smacked the bottom of the carton.

Cold wet ice cream poured over my face.

"Oh, no, let me help YOU," I said. I threw the carton. "Enjoy your butter brickle butt."

"The flagstone," Sam said. "The contest."

"You get the hose. I'll get cleaner," I said.

I ran up the steps and into the kitchen.

My mom was giving Justin a pile of money.

"What's going on?" I asked.

"Nothing," they said at the same time.

I could tell it was something. My ears felt hot and red.

"You're paying him?" I asked. "For what?"

My mom started up with her breathing.

I looked at Justin. "Are you our friend, Justin? Or our babysitter?"

His face was red too. "Your friend," he said.

"Only?" I asked.

"And sort of a babysitter," he said.

"It's not what you think," my mom said.

But it was. And I never felt so bad in my life.

# 23

# THE THIRD PART

*I* ran up two steps at a time, down the hall, and into my room. Then I shut my door.

"Melonhead?" a voice said.

"Go away," I said.

"It's Justin," Justin said. "Your friend."

"You are NOT my friend," I said. "You have NEVER been my friend. You WILL NEVER be my friend."

"Open the door, darling boy," my mom said.

I did not answer.

"I'm leaving," Justin said. "But I'm coming back."

I sat on the radiator cover and looked down at the sidewalk.

"Come out and let me explain," my mom said. "Please."

I was too mad to answer. I could hear her fast breathing. That lasted for over a half hour. Then it was quiet.

The next voice was my dad's. "Sport, Mom called me. I know what happened. I need to come in."

"You're supposed to be at the airport," I said.

"I came back," he said. "I decided to take the five a.m. flight from BWI instead."

That means he has to get up at three in the morning. Plus drive forty-five minutes to the Baltimore airport. It hardly takes eleven minutes to get to Reagan National.

I did not open the door.

"Did you know Justin was a babysitter?" I asked.

"Your mom told me but I don't think I was paying enough attention," he said. "I thought you were fine with Justin, who, by the way, I would call a companion, not a babysitter."

"I brought you a cheese and pickle sandwich," my mom said.

"I don't want it," I said. Even though it's my favorite.

I fished yesterday's shorts from under my bed and sucked Froot Loops powder out of the pocket. I pretended I was a marooned astronaut who had to eat dust to survive.

A piece of paper slid under the door.

"Writing me a letter won't help, Mom," I said.

"I didn't," she said.

I read it.

*Dear Melonhead,*

*When I took the job all I knew about you was that you got stuck in a tree (I saw you) and fell in a fountain (I saw YouTube). I thought you were a chucklehead.*

*But once I got to know you, I liked you, a lot. Sam, too. You're smart and funny. You make me wish I had a little brother.*

*I should have told your mom to forget about paying me, but I like money. (That's how come I could pay for fountain parts.)*

*Is this the worst day of your life? Probably so. I'm sorry for the part that was my fault.*

*If you ever want to hang out (for no charge) call me.*

*Your friend,*

*Justin*


*P.S. I brought you a Venus flytrap. It eats raw hamburger and flies but don't overfeed it.*


I wrote a list on the back of the letter.

1. No forgiveness eve

2. I will not accept the Venus flytrap even though I have always wanted one.

3. Every day I will remind myself to never betray anybody.


"Sport," my dad said. "I'm coming in."

"Okay," I said. "But Mom can't."

He sat next to me on the floor. "Your mom did it because she loves you."

"She doesn't trust me," I said.

"She wants to keep you safe."

"It's the most embarrassing thing that ever happened to me," I told him.

"I can see that," he said.

"I thought he was my friend," I said.

"I think he is," my dad said. "But you'll have to decide for yourself."

We talked until I was ready to go downstairs. That was over one hour. My mom hugged me. "I was wrong. You have a good reason to be mad at me. I'm very sorry."

"I'm forgiving you but not Justin," I said.

At eleven at night, we sat at the kitchen table and ate Betty's Famous Cream Cheese Omelets.

"Listen to that wind," my dad said. "You'd think we were in a Florida hurricane."

"We're in a hurricane?" I said. "Hot diggity."

"No," he said. "But it's more wind than Washington is used to getting."

It sounded like somebody far away was shrieking.

My mom got up to watch. My dad and I stood by her sides. Through the rain we could see delphiniums flying by. And sweet peas. A flowerpot smashed.

My dad gave her a hug.

At ten minutes before midnight the storm was over. So was the garden.

"Mom," I said. "Remember the story of the Terrible, Horrible, No Good, Very Bad Day?"

"Yes," she said.

"We just had it," I said.

# 24

# MY ACCIDENTAL IDEA

When I woke up my mom was already outside in our shambles of a backyard.

"Did the ladybugs survive?" I said.

"The aphids did," she said. "I don't know what they'll eat now that the rosebush is a flowerless stick."

"I'm sorry for you, Mom," I said.

"The sunny side of this disaster is I can take you and Sam to the Big Stink," she said.

"Really?" I said.

She smiled.

"You'll hate it," I said.

"I know," she said. "But you'll love it and I love you, so we'll have a good time."

I hugged her.

"Since I'm suddenly free, I'm driving to Baltimore to see Aunt Cindy," she said. "Do you want to come?"

"I'm going to see if Mrs. Wilkins's plants got beaten to death," I said.

"You are a good boy," she said. "When you're done, go straight to the Alswangs'. You're invited."

"It's a deal," I said. "Have fun in Charm City."

That's what people call Baltimore.

Mrs. Wilkins was on her porch.

"I've been waiting for you," she said.

"How's the jungle?" I asked.

"One fine thing about too many plants packed together is that storms have a hard time uprooting them," Mrs. Wilkins said.

"That's a relief," I said. "I'm going to see the Big Stink tomorrow. My dad can't take us, but since the garden blew away my mom can."

"Bad weather was a good break for you," Mrs. Wilkins said.

"Horrible for my mom," I said.

Then I realized how horrible I felt.

"She worked on it for months," I said. "She had garden tour meetings. She studied growing zones. She made a flower map and spied on Mrs. Hackett's yard. She ordered bugs."

"Can't control nature," Mrs. Wilkins said.

"If I had the power plus a time machine, I'd go back and make the storm skip over our house," I said.

"You'd miss the titan arum," she said.

"I would trade," I said.

"You would?" she asked.

"I'm shocking myself," I told her. "But I think the contest is even more important to my mom than the Big Stink is to me."

"How bad is her garden?" Mrs. Wilkins asked.

"It's mostly mud and puddles. Grasses and morning glory vines are the only things left."

"Get your friends over here," she said. "Tell them not to break anything."

Sam, Jonique, and Lucy Rose came together. I bet they were scared to come one at a time.

"Where's Justin?" Mrs. Wilkins said.

"He's not our friend," I said.

She looked at us. "Roll up your sleeves," she said. "I don't care for lazy children."

"That's true," I told them. "Believe me."

Madam calls Lucy Rose a chatterbox but in front of Mrs. Wilkins she was quiet as a pencil. Ditto for Sam and Jonique. I should have told them Mrs. Wilkins doesn't have what my dad calls follow-through. Usually follow-through is good but when someone says she's going to boil you in oil or string you up by your thumbs, it's a comfort to know she will never get around to it.

"Quit staring at me, Jonique McBee," Mrs. Wilkins said. "Now, all of you, follow me to the back porch."

She dried off the green chair and sat. "You are the workers," she said. "I am the boss."

"You changed your mind about more boys, less work," I said.

"It's not changed yet," she said.

"How come we're here?" Sam asked.

"Don't just stand around like a Christmas tree, Melonhead. Tell them your idea," Mrs. Wilkins said.

"What idea?" I said.

"The storm destroyed Melonhead's mother's garden," she said.

"So we can go to New York!" Sam said.

"Melonhead has decided to skip New York so Mrs. Melon can stay in the contest," Mrs. Wilkins said.

"But she's bound to lose," Lucy Rose said.

"Pay attention," Mrs. Wilkins said. "I don't like repeating myself."

When she finished I said, "Mrs. Wilkins, you can't do this. Your yard is your life."

"I've decided to make my life my life," she said.

Sam looked at me. I shrugged.

"Mr. Wilkins would like that," Mrs. Wilkins said.

"Isn't he dead?" Sam said.

"It's rude to remind her," Lucy Rose said.

"I was recently given a plant that takes care of itself," Mrs. Wilkins said. "I like that."

"Let's get to digging," Sam said.

"Start with the dwarf weeping cherry," Mrs. Wilkins said.

"It's hunched over," Jonique said.

"That's the beauty of it," I told her.

"I would say that's the ugly of it," Lucy Rose whispered.

"I heard that," Mrs. Wilkins said. "You girls start uprooting the *Doodia aspera*."

"I don't know what a *Doodia aspera* is," Lucy Rose said.

"Don't they teach you anything at school?" Mrs. Wilkins said. "Jonique, show Lucy Rose that purple-and-green plant."

"It looks prehistoric," Jonique said.

"It is," Mrs. Wilkins told her.

Sam and Lucy Rose and Jonique got a lot done in two hours. I did not.

"Mrs. Wilkins," I said, "the cherry tree has to stay."

"Impossible," she said. "It's a showstopper. We just need more muscle. Call Justin."

"I'd rather dig with my teeth," I said.

"Well, get to chewing," Mrs. Wilkins said.

Sam and I dug together. "It's stuck," I said.

"Friends are too valuable to throw away," Mrs. Wilkins said.

"Justin turned out to be a crumb," Sam said.

"Even worse, he's a babysitter," I said. "My mom was PAYING him to hang around with us."

Jonique spun her head around so fast, a braid got caught on a thorn. "Justin was pretending to be your friend?" she asked.

"And mine," Sam said.

"FOR MONEY?" Lucy Rose said.

I nodded.

"He should be utterly ashamed," Lucy Rose said. "You should throw him away."

"Did you know Justin before he was your keeper?" Mrs. Wilkins said.

"We had seen each other," I said.

"So he didn't know you before," she said.

"No," I said.

She laughed. "He'd probably have charged double if he did."

If feelings could bleed, mine would have.

"Oh, come on, Melonhead," Mrs. Wilkins said. "That was a joke. You are good company."

"I am?"

"Why would I keep telling you to come around if you weren't?" she said. "Your three days were up a long time ago."

I could feel red ears coming.

"When my husband was sick we had a nurse come to the house to help take care of him. We paid her, of course. After a bit she became a good friend."

"Where is she now?" Sam asked.

"Florida," Mrs. Wilkins said.

"That's different," I said.

"Did Justin regret what he did?" she asked.

"He said he did, in a letter," I told her.

"It takes trouble to write a letter," she said.

"And he gave me a Venus flytrap."

"A useful plant," she said. "How about your mom?"

"She said she made a bad mistake," I said.

"Everyone makes those sometimes," Mrs. Wilkins said.

"Not you," I said. "You let your kids keep a monkey in the house."

"I made other mistakes," she said. "No parent can be perfect. Looking back, the monkey was at least half a mistake."

"Pepe?" I said.

"I've come to think jungle animals shouldn't live in houses," she said. "Also, monkeys are inconvenient. Pepe had a fondness for unscrewing things. We'd go to salt our food and the shaker top would fall off. Dinner would be buried under a mountain of salt."

"If a monkey did that to me, I'd laugh my lips off," Lucy Rose said. "Then I'd get it a job being on TV."

"Once Pepe poured shampoo on the bathroom floor. Andy looked like he was dancing on ice. When he crashed into the toilet, Pepe laughed like a madman."

Mrs. Wilkins laughed more than Pepe.

"Maybe Justin could be like the Wilkinses' nurse," Sam said.

"Maybe not," I said. "Besides, I don't know his phone number."

"You could, if you changed your mind, run around the fence and see if Justin's at Parks and Rec," Mrs. Wilkins said.

"I'm for that," Sam said.

"That is exactly what I do not want to do," I said.

"Think of your mom," Jonique said.

I found Justin playing bumper pool with another teenager. "Melonhead!" he yelled when he saw me. "Come here!"

We met in the middle of the blacktop.

"Hurry up!" his friend yelled.

"I forfeit!" Justin said.

"Come on, Justin," the guy hollered.

"Sorry, man. One of my best friends just got here."

"That kid is your friend?" the guy yelled.

Justin yelled back, "I'm lucky."

"I'm not your friend," I said. "You are my mom's friend. So I came to see if you want to help her or not."

He did.

We had the tree up by two o'clock. I hadn't said one word since the playground.

"Time for lunch," Mrs. Wilkins said. "Come up and eat."

She was holding a half gallon of mint chocolate chip ice cream and six spoons.

# 25
## SHOCK

Mrs. Wilkins had a rest while we pushed a tippy wheelbarrow from one yard to the other.

"I am utterly beat to bits," Lucy Rose said after the last load.

Mrs. Wilkins was refreshed. "Hop to it, people," she said. "We don't have all day."

It was like we were in the army. Mrs. Wilkins was the map reader, we were the diggers.

"Jonique, plant the tall grass along the back of the highest flower bed. Sam can plant the yucca. Yucca's the one that looks like the top of a nuclear pineapple, Sam," Mrs. Wilkins said. "Leave room in front so Lucy Rose can plant a row of *Doodia aspera.* You want to show off the colorful leaves. Justin, dig a hole in the round bed and put in the dwarf cherry tree. Melonhead will give you a hand. When you're done, plant the *Clivia miniata* around the trunk. And Sam, watch it with that hose. I'm old. I could rust."

"Let's do it," Justin said to me.

"Fine," I said, in an unfriendly way.

"I thought palm plants had to live near beaches," Lucy Rose said.

"The *Chamaerops humilis* looks tropical but it's a pretender," Mrs. Wilkins said. "My husband got it in northern Africa. Sam, help her lift it into the flower bed."

"Mrs. Wilkins," Lucy Rose said. "You are looking sad around the edges."

"I'm not sad, Lucy Rose," she said. "When you're old your lips droop."

"Mrs. Melon has stickers for that," Sam told her.

"The tree looks good," I said to Justin. "Thanks."

"That's what friends are for," he said.

I did not answer.

"The resurrection plants go in the empty spaces," Mrs. Wilkins said. "Hide the bowls with mulch. Girls, figure out where those white arums should go."

"Arum?" I asked. "Like titan arum."

"These are little," Sam said.

"They don't stink," Justin said.

"Most arums are like most people," Mrs. Wilkins said. "Average height and decent-smelling."

I felt like we'd worked for a year.

"I've got Gumby arms," Justin said.

"Same for me," I said.

Finally Mrs. Wilkins said, "Go up and take a look from the porch."

"Holy moly," Sam said.

Lucy Rose said, "It's like we're yard fairies."

"I am no yard fairy," I said. I pointed at Sam and a little bit at Justin. "None of us are."

"We did a job, didn't we?" Justin said.

"We did," I told him.

Then I realized. "Hang on," I said, "I've got to get two things."

I put the

bucket fountain on the step above the pot of yellow lilies. Justin plugged in the extension cord.

Mrs. Wilkins slapped her own leg. "I've got to have one of those," she said.

"We'll make you one," Justin said.

I put the Venus flytrap in a clay pot. "In case the judges take off points for flies," I said.

Jonique, Sam, Lucy Rose, and I played Skittles catch in front of my house until we saw my mom parking across the street. "Who's ready for the Big Stink?" she yelled.

When she got closer she said, "You four look like urchins."

"Sea urchins?" Jonique asked.

"Or the raggedy children kind of urchins?" Lucy Rose said.

"Follow me to the urchin den, Mom," I said so she wouldn't suspect. "We washed our feet."

I led her through the house and opened the back door.

"Darling boy," she said. "Seeing the backyard now will make me sad."

"One peek," I said.

"Not now. Maybe . . . My goodness!" my mom said. "I'm stunned."

She looked over the porch railing. "It's beautiful. Unusual! Who did all this work? Where did you get these plants?"

Then she saw Mrs. Wilkins sitting below on the short wall. "Winnie, you came out of the house. And Justin! Winnie, are these your plants?"

"Yours now," Mrs. Wilkins said. "The kids did the work."

"You're back in the contest," I said.

My mom hugged me and Sam and the girls two at a time. "I'm coming down to look at this spectacular garden up close," she said. "Winnie and Justin, prepare to be hugged."

We walked from plant to plant. "I would have never been this creative, this free-form," my mom said. "It's a shining gem of a garden."

"We followed your map," Mrs. Wilkins said. "Same arrangement. Different plants."

"I predict the judges will flip over the bush that looks like it's covered with slug slime," Sam said.

"I'm sure they would," my mom said. "But they'll be skipping our house. I promised the Big Stink. We're leaving at four-thirty tomorrow morning."

"I decided it's better for you to stay here," I said.

"I decided it's better for me to take two boys to New York," she said.

"You have to be here," Jonique said. "The judges are coming."

"Seriously, Mom," I said.

"This is the nicest thing anyone has ever done

for me," my mom said. "But you can't talk me out of the Big Stink."

Everybody stayed to eat hamburgers and green Jell-O in the new backyard.

The unusual thing was that Mrs. Wilkins looked happy.

"I would leave town to see a titan arum," she said.

"Too bad you can't on account of your shaky hips," Lucy Rose said.

"I could go with you," Justin said. Then he looked at me. "No charge."

Mrs. Wilkins looked at Justin. "I've got two rules, buster. Don't be late and don't make me walk all over Manhattan."

"We'll take taxis," Justin said.

My mom got a look of panic.

"Mrs. Melon," Justin said. "Seriously. You said I was responsible. It's a great idea. I'll pay for my ticket with the money you paid me."

"I'll think before I act," I said.

"You'll call me when you get there," my mom said.

"I will."

"Don't eat anything you don't recognize."

"I won't."

"No running ahead."

"I won't even walk fast."

"You'll have to wear nice clothes."

"Deal."

"And keep them clean."

"I will try."

"I don't want you looking—"

"Like an urchin," I said. "I won't."

"Don't wear out Mrs. Wilkins."

"Anything else?"

"No situations!" she said.

"I know, Mom," I said. "They're mature in New York."

"Walk me home, Melonhead," Mrs. Wilkins said. "I need you to run up to the attic."

"Now?" I asked.

"If I wanted you to do it next year, I'd ask you next year," she said.

By the time I got home, my mother had ironed my shirt and pants. "I'm pinning twenty dollars in your pocket in case of emergency," she said.

"We won't be having any," I said.

"You know, this is a huge leap of faith for me," she said.

"Faith in me?" I asked.

"Yes," she said.

"Thank you," I said.

# 26
# THE BIGGEST BUNGA

At five a.m. my mom and I picked up Sam and drove to Mrs. Wilkins's. She was standing in front of the fence, wearing a plaid skirt and an orange jacket with gold buttons and her squishy black shoes.

"Did you see my strictas pin?" she asked my mom.

"It's unusual," my mom said. "And I like your lipstick."

I remembered what my dad said about ladies and compliments. "It makes your teeth look white and not fake at all," I said.

"Adam!" my mom said like she was embarrassed.

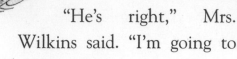

"He's right," Mrs. Wilkins said. "I'm going to wear lipstick more often."

"Your hat is striking," my mom said. "Yellow flowers suit you."

"Thank you," Mrs. Wilkins said. "It took your son days to find my albums but he found my hats in a second."

Justin was a block away and running to us.

"What is he pushing?" Sam asked.

He was sweating when he got to us.

"I rented a wheelchair from Grubb's drugstore, Winnie," my mom said. "Just in case you get tired."

"Waste of money," Mrs. Wilkins said. "I'm not feeble."

We got back to Union Station at nine-thirty at night. My mom was waving from the sidewalk. She hugged me practically in half.

"You're safe and sound," she said.

"Betty, you worry too much," Mrs. Wilkins said.

204

My mom smiled. "You're using the wheelchair, Winnie."

"Pushing me around kept them occupied," Mrs. Wilkins said.

"Mrs. Melon, did you win?" Sam said.

"Later, Sam," my mom said. "I'm about to get a parking ticket."

We ran. Justin and Sam and I folded up the wheelchair and stuffed it in the trunk while my mom explained, "I'm sorry, Officer. I did see the

sign but my little boy would be scared if he didn't see me."

"The one with the red tie tied around his forehead like he's a ninja?"

My mom nodded.

"I know that boy, lady," he said. "He doesn't scare easily."

My mom found a parking place near our house. Lucy Rose, Jonique, Mrs. Alswang, and Baby Julie were inside.

"Tell everything," Lucy Rose demanded.

"Hold on," my mom said. "I know a man who wants to hear the Big Stink report."

Julia pinched her nose. "No Bees tink," she said.

My dad picked up on the first ring.

"You're on speaker," my mom said. "We're all here."

"How was the bunga bangkai, Sport?" he asked.

"You know how some people dream about a trip for weeks and by the time they get there, it's a fat disappointment?" I said.

"I'm sorry that happened," my dad said.

"We had the opposite," I said. "The Big Stink was even bigger and stinkier than I imagined."

"How lucky is that?" Sam said. "Plus, on the way up we made friends with the train conductor."

"He gave me a complimentary throw-up bag for my collection," I said.

"You boys get luckier by the minute," my dad said.

"The trains have bathrooms," Sam said. "I got to pee while we were riding through Philadelphia at sixty miles per hour! Plus the toilets have blue water."

"Toy leet," Julia said. "Toy leet fush!"

"We got to drink all the Coke we wanted because Mrs. Wilkins said she didn't see why not," I said.

"What happened when you got to New York?" Sam's dad asked.

"We took a taxi to the botanical garden," Justin said.

"New York taxis are like police cars," I told

Sam's dad. "There's a plastic divider between the front and the back."

"We only had to wait in line for forty minutes," Mrs. Wilkins said.

"That many people wanted to experience the Big Stink?" my dad asked.

"Of course," I said. "More than a thousand people were behind us."

"When I saw it I felt like I'd fall over from happiness," Sam said.

"How big was it?" Jonique said.

"A station wagon could fit inside the Big Stink," Justin said.

"Great idea," Sam said. "Then you'd have a whole carload of stink."

"You already do have a carload of stink," I said. "From when the moldy banana experiment spread under the seats."

"We took pictures of ourselves in front of the titan arum," Mrs. Wilkins said. "I'm sending them to my children."

"How was the smell?" my dad asked.

"*Much worse* than I expected," I said.

"You expected it to be ghastly," my mom said.

"It was ghastlier," Sam said. "He threw up from it."

"Luckily, I had my souvenir throw-up bag," I said. "The guard said he wished everybody brought them."

My dad yelled through the phone, "Three cheers for Odoardo Beccari!"

"Six cheers for Mrs. Wilkins and Justin," I said.

"Afterward we took the subway," Justin said.

"Melonhead and I escalated to success," Sam said.

"What does that mean?" my mom asked.

"Nothing important," Mrs. Wilkins said. "The interesting part is that the subway took us to Carnegie Deli. Your son needed to refill his stomach."

"I ate so much the waitress said they should name a sandwich after me," I said. "But it might be like stamps and you have to die first. They have a Frank Sinatra.

"I wish you were here for dessert," I told my dad. "Baking Divas made cakes for the House and Garden Tour."

"It's a beaut," Lucy Rose said. "The top is sparkling green with icing flowers and a real red ribbon. It says 'Second Place!' "

"You won second place for the yard?" my dad asked.

"Second place for Most Unusual!" my mom said.

"I'd like to see first place," Mrs. Wilkins said.

"The ribbon has everybody's name on it!" Jonique said.

"Of course," my mom said. "It was a group garden. They loved the H2O4U."

My mom cut the cake. "Adam," she said. "Wash your hands first. They're so dirty you'd think you'd been walking on them."

"Not today," I said.

I was waiting for cake when I said, "I forgot the Scoop du Jour!"

"There's more to this day?" my dad asked.

Mrs. Wilkins said, "After we left the titan arum, your son led us to the office of the man in charge of the botanical garden."

"Did you meet him?" my mom said.

"I almost didn't," I said.

"When Melonhead told the lady in front of the office why he had to meet the director, she said he was too busy," Justin said.

"But the director heard and came out anyway," Sam said.

"What an honor!" my mom said.

"You do make an impression, Sport," my dad said.

"He shook my hand," I told them. "Then he said, 'I am Mr. Pinot. Thank you for stopping by. I have been anxious to meet the person who sent me an envelope full of alpaca poop.' "

Save the date!

THREE YEARS FROM
NOW ANOTHER TITAN
ARUM WILL BE BLOOMING
IN SAN DIEGO. WE'LL BE
THERE. I'VE ALREADY
TAKEN THE TIME OFF.

DAD

Melonhead will tell you how to make your own
floating faucet fountain. Follow along!

**The first things you need are money and a grown-up to help you! When you're ready:**

**GO** to the hardware store and buy one cheap faucet. The lighter it is, the better it is. But it has to be the kind people have on the outside of their house. Once Pop gave me an old faucet that he had to get rid of because the handle wouldn't turn. It was free and I was recycling. That is the best of all deals.

**BUY** one plastic bucket that's about 12 inches tall plus some quick-drying plumber's putty. If you have a used bucket, that's even better. Used plumber's putty is not better. It's useless.

**GO** to a pet store and buy one electric aquarium pump and 24 inches of HARD plastic aquarium tubing that is a half inch wide. Ask the person in charge to make sure it fits on the pump. Do NOT get bendable aquarium tubing. If you do, the fountain will be a flop. Believe me. I know.

**BUY** one bottle of springwater. Do NOT use tap water. It makes deposits that will gunk up the faucet.

**COLLECT** a half a bucketful of decent-size rocks. Gravel is indecent because it's too small.

**FIND** an old plastic bowl or sherbet bucket that is big enough to hold the pump and small enough to fit inside the big bucket. Make sure the pump is not crammed in the bowl—it needs air around it. Also, the sides of the bowl have to be taller than the pump.

## READY? STEADY? GO!

**Step 1:** Stuff the BACK of the faucet with plumber's putty so it's completely sealed up. Make sure no putty sticks out. The front part of the faucet, where the water comes out, has to stay empty. These are two important things.

**Step 2:** Put the aquarium tubing on the aquarium pump. It will stick straight up.

**Step 3:** Put the pump inside the bowl or small bucket.

**Step 4:** Cut a hole in the side of the big bucket, near the bottom. My mom says this is no job for a boy, so get a parent or somebody as old as Justin.

**Step 5:** Put the bowl with the pump inside the big bucket. Do not make a hole in the small bucket, just drape the plug cord over the side. Then poke the pump's plug out through the hole in the big bucket.

**Step 6:** Pour water into the inside bowl. Don't worry about the pump. It's waterproof.

**Step 7:** Gently put enough rocks inside the big bucket so that they cover up the pump and the inside bowl and the space surrounding the inside bowl. When you are done it should look like a bucket of rocks with a plastic tube sticking up like a flagpole.

**Step 8:** When the plumber's putty is as hard as cement, put the tube inside the front of the faucet.

**Step 9:** Put the holey side of the bucket and the plug in the back so people can't see them.

**Step 10:** Plug the aquarium pump into a nearby electrical outlet.

**Step 11:** Find an audience to impress.

**Step 12:** Get congratulated for being a genius!

# ABOUT THE AUTHOR

Like Melonhead, Katy Kelly grew up in Washington, D.C., on Capitol Hill, five blocks away from the United States Capitol. Both love adventures, visiting New York City, and having a hilarious friend named Lucy Rose. Unlike Melonhead, Katy Kelly does not enjoy rodents, hanging off the roof, or things that stink.

Katy Kelly lives with her artist husband and their daughters, Emily and Marguerite. This is her sixth book for young readers and the second in the Melonhead series.

# ABOUT THE ILLUSTRATOR

Gillian Johnson and her family lived for ten years in Tasmania, Australia, a place far from Capitol Hill where there are many fascinating and exotic plants.

Gillian Johnson now lives in Oxford, England, with her husband and two sons and has a wonderful garden.